Tom Jones

HENRY FIELDING

Level 6

Retold by Janet McAlpin
Series Editors: Andy Hopkins and Jocelyn Potter

Pearson Education Limited
Edinburgh Gate, Harlow,
Essex CM20 2JE, England
and Associated Companies throughout the world.

ISBN 0 582 36414 0

First published in 1749
Published in Penguin Popular Classics 1994
This edition first published 1999

Fourth impression 2000

Text copyright © Janet McAlpin 1999
Illustrations copyright © David Cuzik (Pennant Illustration) 1999

Typeset by Digital Type, London
Set in 11/14pt Bembo
Printed in Spain by Mateu Cromo, S.A. Pinto (Madrid)

Published by Pearson Education Limited in association with
Penguin Books Ltd., both companies being subsidiaries of Pearson Plc

Contents

Introduction

To be honest, it was the opinion of all Mr Allworthy's family that young Tom was born to be hanged. Indeed I am sorry to say there was too much reason for this. From his earliest years, Tom showed signs of crime.

When the good – and very rich – Mr Allworthy finds a baby boy in his bed, he decides to keep him, and gives him the name Tom Jones. Tom has a very happy childhood and loves Mr Allworthy dearly, but he finds it hard to keep out of trouble. However, Mr Allworthy always forgives Tom until his nephew Blifil interferes and turns Mr Allworthy against the young man.

Tom is sent away from home, but not before he has fallen deeply in love with his neighbour's daughter, the lovely Sophia Western, and she with him. Now that the young man has no chance of receiving money from Mr Allworthy, though, Sophia's father will not allow them to be together.

While Tom travels along the roads of eighteenth-century England, Sophia – a very determined young lady – leaves home too, in an attempt to escape marriage to the hateful Blifil. Will Tom manage to stay out of trouble for long enough to win his bride? Or will their enemies succeed in keeping the young lovers apart?

Henry Fielding was born in 1707 in Somerset in the west of England. His mother died when he was still a boy and his father sent him away to be educated privately at Eton College.

At the age of twenty-two Fielding moved to London and made a living by writing for the stage. In the eight years between 1729 and 1737 he wrote twenty-five plays. Although many of them were very successful, he is best known for *Tom Thumb*, which was first performed in 1730 and appeared in book form the following year. *Tom Thumb* is a comedy in which Fielding makes fun of other dramatists of the time; at the end of the play there are nine deaths in under a minute and no character is left alive.

Fielding also made fun of politics and politicians in his plays, but the government of the time was not amused. In 1737 a new law was introduced which banned plays like his, and Fielding's career as a dramatist and theatre manager came to an end. He then turned his attention to the study of law and became a lawyer. At the same time he practised journalism, and he became the editor of a newspaper called *The Champion*, in which he could continue to express his views.

It was in this later part of his life that Fielding began to write novels. These are often considered to be the first modern novels written in English, and they were a great influence on later writers like Dickens and Thackeray. Although *Amelia* (1751) was Fielding's biggest-selling novel, it is *The History of Tom Jones, A Foundling*, which appeared in 1749, that readers still find most amusing and relevant two hundred and fifty years later.

While he was writing, Fielding also worked as a well-known and powerful legal official and he fought throughout his life to improve levels of honesty and fairness in the legal system. But he was becoming very ill. In 1754 he travelled to Portugal in the hope of some improvement to his health, but died in Lisbon that same year. His last book, *The Journal of a Voyage to Lisbon* (1755), which he called 'a novel without a plot', was published a year after his death. Fielding was married twice, and Sophia Western is said to share many of the qualities of his first wife, who died after ten years of marriage.

Tom Jones appeared in six volumes and it was enthusiastically received by its readers. Ten thousand copies were sold in the first nine months, and by the end of the century the novel was available in six other European languages. The story had also become a stage play. The story mixes love, adventure and comedy against the background of the colourful times of King George II. The plot is fast and dramatic, many of the characters are highly entertaining, and the adventures of the book's energetic hero keep us amused to the end.

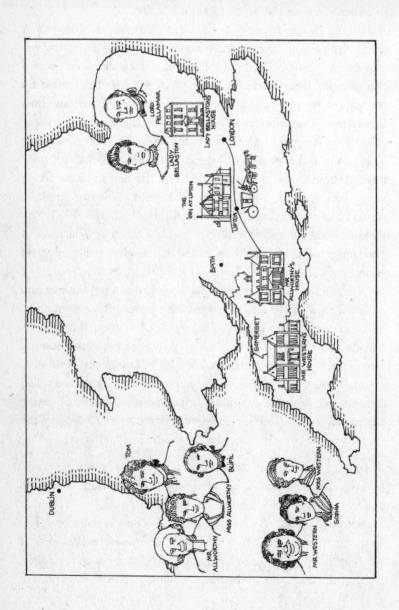

Chapter 1 A Baby is Found

In the west of England, in a part of the country called Somerset, there lived a gentleman whose name was Allworthy. He might be called the favourite of both Nature and Fortune, because Nature had given him the gifts of good health, good sense and a kind heart, and Fortune had made him one of the richest landowners in that part of England.

In his youth this gentleman had married a good, beautiful woman. They had three children, all of whom died young, and about five years before this story begins his wife also died. He loved her still, and sometimes said that he was waiting to join her after death.

He now lived in the country most of the time, with his sister, Miss Bridget Allworthy. This lady was now past the age of thirty. She was a very good woman who often thanked God she was not beautiful, because she believed that beauty led women into wicked ways.

Now, reader, as Mr Allworthy had a large fortune, a good heart and no family, you may think that he lived an honest life, gave to the poor, built a hospital and died a rich man. It is true that he did many of these things, but they are not the reason for this story. Something much more extraordinary happened.

One evening, Mr Allworthy came back to his house very late and very tired. He had been away in London on business for several months. After a light supper with his sister, he went to bed. First he spent some time on his knees, praying to God, and then he pulled back the bedclothes. To his great surprise he saw a baby lying in his bed in a sweet, deep sleep. He stood for some time, looking at its innocent beauty, and then rang his bell to call his elderly housekeeper, Mrs Deborah Wilkins.

When Mrs Wilkins saw the child she cried out, 'My good sir! What shall we do?' Mr Allworthy answered that she must take care of the child that evening, and in the morning he would give orders to find a nurse for it.

'Yes sir,' said Mrs Wilkins, 'and I hope you will give orders to send its wicked mother to prison for doing this.'

'In leaving the baby here, Deborah,' said Mr Allworthy, 'I suppose the poor woman has tried to provide a good home for her child, and I am very glad she has not done worse.'

'But sir,' cried Mrs Wilkins, 'why should you take care of the child? Why not put it in a basket and leave it at the church door? If you keep it people may think that you are the father.'

But Mr Allworthy did not hear her. He now had one of his fingers in the sweet child's hand, and was smiling at it gently. So Mrs Wilkins took the child to her room, and Mr Allworthy went to bed and slept well until morning.

◆

Mr Allworthy's house stood on a hill and had a charming view of the valley beneath. To the right of the valley were several villages, and to the left a great park. Beyond the park the country gradually rose into a range of wild mountains, the tops of which were above the clouds.

The house was very noble. It was surrounded by a fine garden, with old oak trees and a stream that flowed down to a lake at the bottom of the hill. From every room at the front of the house you could see the lake, and a river that passed for several miles through woods and fields till it emptied itself into the sea.

It was now the middle of May, and as Mr Allworthy stood watching the sun rise over this lovely view, Miss Bridget Allworthy rang her bell and called him to breakfast.

When she had poured the tea, Mr Allworthy told his sister he had a present for her. She thanked him. This was not unusual as he often gave her new clothes and jewellery to wear. Imagine her surprise when Mrs Wilkins produced the baby!

Miss Bridget was silent until her brother had told her the whole story. He ended by saying that he had decided to take care of the child and bring it up as his own.

Miss Bridget looked kindly at the child, and told her brother she admired his generosity. He was a good man. However, she was less kind about the poor, unknown mother, whom she called every bad name she could think of. The next step was to discover who the mother was. Mr Allworthy, leaving this task to his housekeeper, and the child to his sister, left the room.

Mrs Wilkins waited for a sign from Miss Bridget. Did she really agree with her brother? Miss Bridget looked for some time at the child as it lay asleep in Mrs Wilkins's lap, then gave it a big kiss, exclaiming about its beauty and innocence. When Mrs Wilkins saw this, she too started squeezing and kissing the baby, and cried out, 'Oh, the dear little child! The dear, sweet, pretty child! He is as fine a boy as I have ever seen.'

Then Miss Bridget gave orders for the servants to get a very good room in the house ready for the child, and to provide him with everything he needed. She was as generous as if he had been a child of her own.

◆

Later that day, Mrs Wilkins went to the village nearby to ask questions about the abandoned child. She soon decided that the most likely mother was Jenny Jones.

Jenny Jones was a poor young girl from the village who had lived as a servant with a schoolmaster and his wife for several years. She had a quick mind and a desire to learn, so the schoolmaster had helped to educate her. Jenny became proud of her learning, and when she returned to the village she behaved in a superior way, which her neighbours hated.

They also noticed that Jenny had often been to Mr Allworthy's house. She had nursed Miss Bridget in a recent illness, and had sat up many nights looking after her. Indeed, Mrs Wilkins herself had seen Jenny at the house the very day before Mr Allworthy's return. She hurried back to the house to tell Mr Allworthy her suspicions.

Mr Allworthy called Jenny to the house. She confessed freely to being the baby's mother, but she refused to name the father.

'I thank you, sir, for your kindness to my poor helpless child,' she said. 'He is innocent, and I hope he will live to be grateful for your generosity. But sir, on my knees I must ask you not to insist on finding out the name of his father. I have sworn before God not to tell anyone his name now, but I promise that one day you will know.'

Mr Allworthy fully believed all that Jenny told him, and sent her away with the promise that he would not send her to prison, but would help her to lead a better life.

'She was lucky!' said one neighbour, when Jenny returned to the village. A second cried, 'See what it is to be a favourite.' A third, 'Ah, it's because she has education!'

Soon, through the care and goodness of Mr Allworthy, Jenny left the village, and there was more gossip. The villagers decided that Mr Allworthy was the baby's father, and began to feel sorry for Jenny Jones. Some even said he had been cruel to send her away. But the good Mr Allworthy did not listen. Baby Jones stayed in his house and was given Mr Allworthy's first name, which was Thomas.

And now we must leave Jenny Jones and little Tom Jones for a while, as we have much more important things to tell.

Chapter 2 The Shame of Mr Partridge

Mr Allworthy's house and his heart were open to all men, but particularly to men of learning. Though he had not had the

4

advantage of a good education, he had made up for this through wide reading and conversation. Well-educated men were always welcome at his table.

One guest of this kind was Captain Blifil. This gentleman was about thirty-five years of age. After a good education he had joined the king's army, but recently he had left the army and had come to Somerset to live a quiet country life. He liked to study the Bible.

Miss Bridget had read many books about religion, and she often talked to the captain on this subject. Her conversation was so pure, her looks so wise and her manner so serious that she seemed like a saint. Yet soon the captain could see that she was falling in love with him.

Everyone will fall in love once in their lives, and there is no particular age for this, but at Miss Bridget's age love is serious and steady. It was not the captain's body, which was big and rough, nor his face, which was covered up to his eyes by a black beard, but his conversation which charmed her.

As soon as the captain saw this, he returned her affections. To be plain, he was already in love with Mr Allworthy's house, gardens, villages and farms. His sister was no beauty, but as Mr Allworthy had no son, the captain would marry Miss Bridget even if she was the ugliest woman in the world. And, in less than a month, he did just that.

Mr Allworthy did not object to the marriage.

'My sister is many years younger than me,' he thought, 'but she is old enough to make her own decisions. He is a gentleman, and though he is not perhaps her equal in fortune, he is a man of sense and honour, and I have nothing against him. I do not doubt that they love each other, and love is the best basis for marriage.'

◆

Reader, this is not a newspaper, consisting of just the same number of words whether there be any news in it or not. In these pages you will find only the important events, so do not be surprised if sometimes time seems to stand still, and sometimes to fly. We fly now to the time when a fine son was born to Captain and Mrs Blifil.

Though the birth of a son to his dear sister gave great joy to Mr Allworthy, it did not take away his love for the abandoned child to whom he was now godfather. He continued to visit little Tom at least once a day in his room.

Mr Allworthy suggested to his sister that the two boys be raised together in his house. Mrs Blifil agreed, but Captain Blifil was not so easily pleased. He liked to use Bible texts to tell Mr Allworthy that bastard children should be punished. Mr Allworthy disagreed. He said that however guilty the parents might be, their children were certainly innocent, and God would not punish the innocent.

While Captain Blifil was becoming more and more jealous of Mr Allworthy's love for little Tom, Mrs Wilkins made a discovery. She believed she now knew the name of Tom's father.

♦

My reader may remember that Jenny Jones had lived for some years with a certain schoolmaster. His name was Partridge, and he was a pleasant, humorous fellow, but his wife was not. Perhaps this was because, after nine years of marriage, she was still childless.

Mrs Partridge, a jealous woman, had chosen Jenny Jones to be her servant because she was plain, and Jenny lived quietly in their house for more than four years, doing her work and learning Latin from Mr Partridge.

Then, one day, Mrs Partridge saw Jenny sitting closely with her husband studying their books, and suddenly her jealous thoughts began. They were fed by small suspicions, one after another, and soon she lost her temper and ordered Jenny to leave the house.

Mr Partridge, who was afraid of his wife, said nothing, and soon the house was calm again. Mrs Partridge loved her husband and she might have forgotten all about it, but some months later she heard news of Jenny from the village gossips.

'She's had two bastard babies,' they said. 'Their father must be from here, because it's less than nine months since she left the village.'

Mrs Partridge was shocked, and all her jealousy returned. She was convinced of her husband's guilt, and went straight home. The fight which followed was furious. Mrs Partridge attacked her husband with tongue, teeth and hands. Though Partridge did nothing, there was soon blood on both of them. The neighbours came to watch, and soon everyone was saying that Mr Partridge had beaten his wife most cruelly.

The cause of this quarrel was reported in various ways. Some said one thing, others said another, and it was a long time before Mrs Wilkins heard the true reason. When she did, she told Captain Blifil. The captain told Mr Allworthy and Mr Allworthy sent Mrs Wilkins to find Mr Partridge. Though he lived fifteen miles away, Mrs Wilkins went quickly, and brought back the schoolmaster and his wife.

♦

Mr Allworthy began the trial immediately, and it took three days. On the first day, Partridge declared his innocence, but his wife gave all the reasons why she thought him guilty. Partridge was silent, until at last he asked Mr Allworthy to send for Jenny Jones. Mr Allworthy sent a messenger to get Jenny, who now lived a whole day's journey from his house. On the third day everyone came to hear Mr Allworthy's judgement.

Unfortunately, the messenger had returned without Jenny. She had left her new home just a few days earlier, in the company of a soldier.

Mr Allworthy's good opinion of Jenny was now lost for ever. He listened again to Mrs Partridge, who now swore she had discovered her husband and Jenny in bed together, and then he found poor Mr Partridge guilty.

Mr Partridge lost his little school, and soon he lost his wife too for she died suddenly. Though the villagers now began to feel sorry for him, he decided to go away.

♦

Although Mr Allworthy had punished the father, he grew fonder of little Tommy. This did not please Captain Blifil, who saw every example of Mr Allworthy's generosity to others as his own loss.

The captain's greatest pleasure was planning what to do with Mr Allworthy's wealth. He fully expected Mr Allworthy to die soon, leaving his wealth to his sister's son. The captain wanted to make great changes to the house and park, and he spent many hours reading about architecture and gardening. But Fortune was unkind to him. The unlucky captain died first, of a sudden and unexpected accident.

Chapter 3 Young Tom Causes Some Anxiety

The reader will not be surprised if we pass quickly over twelve years when nothing interesting happened. We shall now meet our hero, Tom, at about fourteen years of age.

To be honest, it was the opinion of all Mr Allworthy's family that young Tom was born to be hanged. Indeed I am sorry to say there was too much reason for this. From his earliest years, Tom showed signs of crime. To give three examples, he had stolen some apples from a tree, a duck from a farm and a ball from the pocket of his companion, young Master Blifil.

In contrast, the young son of Captain and Mrs Blifil was

praised by all the neighbourhood. He was quiet and good, and many people wondered why Mr Allworthy allowed his nephew to be educated with such a bad influence as Tom.

Yet Tom, bad as he is, must be our hero, so here is a story to help you to get to know him better.

About this time, Tom had only one friend among the servants, and this was Mr Allworthy's gamekeeper, George Seagrim. Some said that Tom learned his bad ways from this man, whose idea of the meaning of 'yours' and 'mine' was rather loose. Indeed, the whole duck and most of the stolen apples were eaten by Black George and his family.

One day, young Tom went shooting with the gamekeeper near the edge of Mr Allworthy's land. They surprised some birds, which flew into the neighbour's land. Tom ran after them, the gamekeeper followed him and they both fired their guns.

The neighbour, who was riding nearby, heard the gunfire and came to look. He caught Tom with a dead bird, but he didn't find the gamekeeper, who was hiding in the trees.

When he returned home, Tom admitted his crime to Mr Allworthy, but he insisted that he had been shooting alone. The gamekeeper was sent for, but he too denied being with Tom that afternoon. Mr Allworthy sent Tom to bed, and next morning he called him back and asked the same questions. Tom gave the same answers, even when he was whipped.

At last Mr Allworthy believed Tom was telling the truth. He apologized, and gave Tom a little horse as a present.

'Oh, sir,' Tom said, 'you are too good to me.' He very nearly told Mr Allworthy the truth, but then he remembered the gamekeeper and was silent. He felt very guilty.

◆

The thing which put an end to Tom's silence was a fight between himself and Master Blifil. Usually, Tom avoided fights with his younger companion because he really loved him, but one day, as they played together, Blifil called Tom a poor bastard. Tom immediately jumped on Blifil, and the result was a bloody nose.

Blifil ran to his uncle to complain. Tom told Mr Allworthy what Blifil had called him, but young Blifil said, 'He is lying, Uncle, the same way as he lied when he said nobody was with him when he shot the bird. Black George, the gamekeeper, was there. Tom confessed it to me.'

'Is this true, child?' asked Mr Allworthy. 'Why did you lie to me about it?'

Tom explained that it was a question of honour. He had promised the gamekeeper to keep quiet. 'It was my idea to follow the birds, sir,' he said. 'Please, sir, let me be punished. Take my little horse away. But please, sir, forgive poor George.'

Mr Allworthy was quiet for some time. Then he told the boys to go away, and to be more friendly with each other. Towards the gamekeeper he was more severe. He called him to the house, paid him his wages and dismissed him.

◆

The education of Tom and Master Blifil was in the hands of two men, Mr Thwackum and Mr Square, who lived in the house as part of the family. Mr Thwackum knew a lot about religion and morality, while Mr Square had studied philosophy and believed in reason more than in religion.

Mrs Blifil, now many years widowed, liked them both. She enjoyed the conversation of Mr Thwackum, and admired the good looks of Mr Square. Both men had their eye on the possibility of marrying her, and so they hated each other. But there was one point on which they agreed. In order to please the widow, they both took every opportunity to show her that they preferred her son. Poor Tom therefore suffered many more beatings than young Master Blifil.

The good Mr Allworthy called Tom his own boy, and in all things made him equal with Master Blifil. Mrs Blifil agreed with this, though everyone believed she secretly hated Tom. When he was young this may have been so. However, as he grew up and began to learn how to be charming to ladies, she grew fonder of him. By the time he was eighteen years old the whole country was talking of Mrs Blifil's liking for Tom, which made his two teachers hate him even more.

◆

Tom worried greatly about Black George Seagrim and his unfortunate family, and tried to help them. First he sold his little horse to give them money for food, then he sold a fine Bible which Mr Allworthy had given him. He was punished for this with more beatings.

At the same time, Tom began to grow friendly with the neighbour whose dead bird had caused so much trouble, and so he met his neighbour's daughter. But as this young lady is to be the heroine of our story, and probably we will all fall in love with her, it is not right to introduce her at the end of a chapter.

Chapter 4 Tom Falls in Love

Bring on flowers, soft winds and sweet birdsong to welcome the lovely Sophia Western. To imagine her appearance you must think of famous beauties in art and history, and of the woman who is dearest to your own heart.

Sophia was the only daughter of Mr Western. She was now seventeen. Her hair was rich and black, her shape delicate, her eyes bright, her nose regular, her teeth white, her lips red and her neck long and lovely.

Such was the outside of Sophia, and inside she was equally

fine. Her mind was as charming as her appearance, and her sweet temper lit up her face when she smiled.

Sophia had been educated under the care of an aunt, who was a lady of the world. In her manner and conversation, Sophia was a perfect lady. Perhaps she needed a little of the style that comes from life in the highest circles, but style can never replace true innocence and good sense.

Her father was fonder of Sophia than of any other human being, but he allowed his sister to take her away for three years for the sake of her education. Now she had returned, to rule her father's house and to sit at the top of his table, where Tom often dined.

Mr Western had a great love of hunting, and Tom became a favourite companion in this sport. Mr Western often wished he had a son like Tom, and let him freely use everything that was most precious to him: his guns, his dogs and his horses. Tom wanted to ask Mr Western if he would employ Black George. He decided to ask Sophia to help him.

◆

Now if Sophia had some influence on her father, who loved her above all things (after those things already mentioned which he needed for his sport), then Tom had some influence on Sophia.

Tom was now approaching the age of twenty. He was open-hearted, good-natured and had a natural way with ladies. The women of the neighbourhood thought he was a handsome fellow, and so did Sophia.

Tom was also a great favourite of Mr Western, who was so busy with his dogs and his horses that he gave Tom every opportunity to be with his daughter that a lover could wish for. In Tom's company, the innocent Sophia was at her brightest. Tom did not notice this, and it is not surprising, since Sophia did not notice it herself. Indeed, her heart was lost before she suspected it was in danger.

One afternoon, finding Sophia alone, Tom said he had something to ask her. Nature whispered something in Sophia's ear, and the colour left her cheeks. Tom did not notice, and he told her about the gamekeeper, whose unfortunate family was now nearly starving. Would Sophia ask her father to employ Black George?

'I will do it with all my heart,' said Sophia, with a smile full of sweetness. 'I really pity the poor fellow and just yesterday I sent his wife some money and a dress. And now, Mr Jones, I have something to ask you.'

'Anything, madam,' said Tom, taking Sophia's hand and kissing it.

This was the first time his lips had ever touched her, and the blood which before had left her cheeks now rushed back to colour all her face and neck. When she could speak (which was not instantly) Sophia asked Tom not to lead her father through so many dangers when hunting. She was frightened every time they went out together, knowing that Mr Western would follow Tom anywhere. Tom promised not to ride so madly, and left, happy with his success.

That evening, after dinner, Sophia played music for her father. She played all his favourite tunes three times over, and this so pleased the good man that he got up from his chair to give her a kiss. Sophia took this opportunity to keep her promise to Tom. She did it so well that, next morning, the gamekeeper was called and given a job.

Tom's success in this affair was soon widely known. Some said it was an act of good nature. Blifil, who hated Black George, said it was an insult to Mr Allworthy. Thwackum and Square agreed because they were now very jealous of Tom and the widow. But Mr Allworthy approved. He said he wished he could see more examples of such good and loyal friendship.

Fortune had other ideas, however, and soon Mr Allworthy saw Tom's actions in a different light.

♦

Now, though Tom greatly liked Sophia, appreciating her beauty and admiring all her other qualities, she had made no deep impression on his heart. The truth is, it belonged to another woman. This was not Mrs Blifil, though she was clearly fond of Tom. No, it was a younger woman.

The reader will remember that we have often mentioned the family of the gamekeeper, George Seagrim, or Black George, as he was usually called. This family consisted of a wife and five children. The second child was a daughter whose name was Molly. She was considered one of the best-looking girls in the whole country.

When she was sixteen, Tom, who was three years older, began to notice Molly's beauty. Though he was strongly attracted to her, he believed it was wrong to make love to a girl, even a poor girl, and so he stayed away from her house for three whole months. But when Molly saw that Tom was backward, she became more forward, and found a way to meet him and tempt him to do what they both wanted.

Tom desired Molly and Molly gave herself to Tom. Tom was grateful to Molly and wanted to be kind to her. This was the situation. Poor as she was, Tom could not think of abandoning Molly, and so he did not think of loving Sophia.

♦

It was Molly's mother who first noticed the change in her shape. To hide the signs of the baby Molly was expecting, she gave her the dress which Sophia had sent her. Molly, who usually wore rags, was very pleased with the fine dress and wore it to church.

'Who is she?' was the question that ran around the church

Molly, who usually wore rags, was very pleased with the fine dress and wore it to church.

when the fine lady arrived, but when the answer came, 'It's Molly Seagrim', the jealous women laughed at her.

Sophia happened to be present at this time. She was very pleased with the beauty of the girl, and sorry that people laughed at her. When she returned home she called for the gamekeeper and offered to give Molly a job. Poor Seagrim was silent, because he knew about Molly's condition.

Back at the church, an angry scene had developed. As people left they laughed and pointed at Molly's fine dress, and some began to throw dirt and rubbish. Molly turned to face the crowd, and soon a fight broke out among the gravestones. Men and women, but mostly women, bit and scratched and hit and tore at Molly's hair. Clothes were torn too, until many were nearly naked. Molly fought back furiously, with all her strength.

At this point Tom came riding past, with Square and Master Blifil. Seeing his Molly under attack, Tom jumped off his horse and went among the crowd with a horsewhip, turning them away. He then pulled off his coat and buttoned it around Molly, wiped the blood from her face with his handkerchief and took her home on his horse. He gave her a kiss, said he would return in the evening, and rode away.

Chapter 5 A Sleepless Night for Sophia

The next morning Tom went hunting with Mr Western, and afterwards was invited to dinner.

The lovely Sophia was brighter than usual that day, and if she wanted Tom to notice her, she certainly succeeded.

Another dinner guest was Mr Supple, the priest from the village church. He was a good-natured man who was always silent at table, though his mouth was never shut. In other words, he had one of the best appetites in the world. After dinner, though, he loved to talk, and he had some news.

'I believe, lady, you saw a young woman at church yesterday, wearing one of your own dresses. After you left, this dress caused a terrible battle. This morning the young woman in question was called to explain the matter to Mr Allworthy. When she appeared, everyone could see that she will soon give birth to a bastard. As she refused to name the father, she will be sent to prison.'

'Is that your news?' cried Western. 'Nothing more important? Come, Tommy, drink up and pass the bottle.'

Tom made a polite excuse and quickly left the table.

'Aha,' said Western, after he had gone. 'I see, I see! Tom is certainly the father of this bastard.'

'I should be very sorry if that is true,' said Supple.

'Why sorry?' cried Western. 'Haven't you been the father of any bastards yourself? You must have been lucky, then.'

'I am sure you joke, Mr Western,' replied the priest. 'And I hope you are wrong about the young gentleman. He is a little wild, perhaps, but a good young man. I would not like to see him lose the good opinion of Mr Allworthy.'

'No, no,' said Western. 'He will lose nobody's good opinion, and the women will like him better. Ask my daughter here. You have no worse opinion of a young man for giving a girl a bastard, have you, Sophy?'

It was a cruel question to ask poor Sophia. She had seen Tom's colour change when he heard the news, and she thought her father's suspicions were correct. Her heart at once told her the great secret it had been hiding. Shocked and confused, she excused herself and went to her room.

◆

Tom hurried home, and found Molly was still there. He asked for a private conversation with Mr Allworthy, and said he was the guilty father. He begged Mr Allworthy to let Molly return to her family.

After hesitating for some time, Mr Allworthy agreed. He then spoke for a long time about right and wrong. Tom listened gratefully, and promised to improve.

Mr Allworthy was certainly angry with Tom, but he was also pleased with his honour and honesty, so Thwackum could not persuade him to punish the young man.

Square was more clever. He reminded Mr Allworthy of all the things Tom had done for the gamekeeper and his family.

'Now we can see, sir, that these things were not done out of friendship, but to get Molly for his wicked ways.'

For the first time, the good Mr Allworthy began to have a bad impression of Tom.

♦

That night, Sophia slept very little. She was already dressed when her maid, Mrs Honour, came to wake her.

'Oh, madam,' said Mrs Honour, 'what do you think?' And with these words she began to tell Sophia all the gossip from the village about Tom and Molly.

What passed through poor Sophia's mind? The reader will remember that only yesterday the news of Molly had opened Sophia's eyes to her heart's love. Now she decided she felt nothing for Tom. But love is a disease, and the very next time she saw him all her former feelings returned. From that time her heart kept changing from hot to cold to hot again until Sophia was desperate for a cure.

She decided to avoid Tom, and made plans to visit her aunt, but Fortune stopped the plan with an accident.

♦

Every day, Mr Western grew fonder of his daughter, almost more than his precious dogs. Since he could not bring himself to abandon the dogs, he managed cleverly to enjoy both dogs and daughter by taking Sophia hunting with him.

Sophia disliked the sport, which was too rough for her, but she always obeyed her father. She decided not to visit her aunt until the end of the hunting season.

The second time she went hunting her horse started to behave badly. Tom was nearby, and saw that she was in danger. He quickly rode up, jumped off his horse, and was in time to catch Sophia as her horse threw her and ran off.

'Are you hurt, madam?' he asked her. When she said she was unhurt he said, 'Then heaven be praised. If I have broken my arm it is nothing, after the danger you were in.'

'Broken your arm!' screamed Sophia.

'I am afraid I have, madam,' said Tom. 'But I still have a good arm to help you home.'

Mr Western then came back with the other riders and Sophia's horse. Finding his daughter unhurt he was delighted, and everyone returned to the house, where a doctor was called to look at Tom's arm.

This brave act of Tom's made a deep impression on Sophia's heart, and she no longer wanted to visit her aunt.

Chapter 6 Tom Learns a Little about Women

After his accident, Tom stayed at Mr Western's house. He had many visitors. Mr Allworthy came every day, and took the opportunity to give Tom good advice. Thwackum also came and said that heaven was punishing Tom for his bad ways. Square said the opposite, that even a wise man can break an arm. Blifil sometimes came too. But Mr Western was never out of the sickroom, except when he was busy with his horses or his bottle. He told Tom loudly that beer was the best medicine, but the doctor disagreed.

When Tom could sit up, Mr Western brought Sophia to see him. Soon they were free to spend hours together, talking and playing music. Sophia's lips said nothing about her feelings, but her eyes said everything.

One day, Mr Western said to Tom, 'I love you dearly, my boy, and will do anything in my power for you. Tomorrow morning, take your choice of all of my horses. Why not take the young horse that Sophy rode? She cost me fifty pounds.'

'If she cost a thousand pounds,' cried Tom, 'I would give that horse to the dogs.'

'What?' answered Western. 'Because she broke your arm? She's just an animal. Be a man, Tom. Forgive and forget!'

Sophia's face changed as she listened. She believed she knew why Tom hated the horse. Tom noticed her colour, and at last he began to suspect the reason. His heart told him clearly that he loved Sophia, and that she loved him.

♦

Sweet and delicious feelings now filled Tom's heart, but they were mixed with bitter thoughts. He knew that Sophia's father had a violent affection for his daughter, and wanted the best marriage for her. He also knew that fortune, not friendship, would guide Mr Western to a husband for Sophia.

Then there was Molly. Tom and Molly had sworn to love each other, and Molly said she would die if Tom deserted her. Tom imagined her dead, and was shocked. He could not desert her. Then he remembered her youth, health and beauty and desired her again.

With these thoughts, Tom passed a sleepless night. In the morning he had decided to stay with Molly and to think no more of Sophia. But in the afternoon, when he saw Sophia again, the god of Love marched in and won the battle.

♦

Tom now wondered if Molly would be satisfied with a sum of money. She was poor and proud of her beauty, and though she loved Tom she might be happy to be richer than her equals.

One day, with his arm in a bandage, Tom visited Molly. Her mother and sisters said she was upstairs, asleep. Tom climbed the ladder to his fair one's room and found the door locked. He knocked. After some time, she opened it.

They kissed. Then Tom sat Molly on the bed and began to speak. He told her that Mr Allworthy had forbidden him to see her again. Silence. He said that they must separate. More silence. Then he said that he would do everything he could to help her, perhaps even find her a husband.

Molly was silent a little longer, then she began to cry and shout. 'Is this your love for me?' she cried. 'You are false, Tom Jones, like any man!'

She stood up angrily and waved her arms about. Suddenly, by accident, her arm pulled down a curtain beside the bed. Behind the curtain were a few small things belonging to Molly, and . . . a man! It was Mr Square. He was quite naked.

Reader, I am sure you are as surprised as Mr Jones. But why? Even teachers are made of flesh and blood.

Mr Square had admired Molly when he saw her fighting outside the church, and when Tom was sick he went to visit her. It is true that Molly preferred Tom, but Mr Square brought her presents that softened her heart.

And what did Tom do? He laughed. 'I promise I will never speak of this,' he told Square. 'Be kind to the girl and I will never open my lips to anyone. And Molly, be true to your friend and I will forgive you for being false to me.'

Then Tom climbed quickly down the ladder and left the house. One of Molly's sisters followed him.

'Sir,' she said. 'Now that you know about Mr Square, I have something else to tell you. You were not the first man to make love to Molly. It was Will Barnes. Will is the father of Molly's bastard.'

◆

The secret about Molly made Tom's heart feel light, but it was full of violent storms when he thought about Sophia. He loved her madly, and plainly saw her tender feelings for him, but her father would never accept him for her husband.

Tom struggled with his love. He did not want to offend his good friend Mr Western, or his godfather Mr Allworthy. The battle made him sick and sad. When Sophia came near he became pale, and when her eyes met his, the blood rushed into his cheeks. Mr Western noticed nothing, but Sophia saw and understood, because she felt the same.

One day, the young couple met, by accident, in the garden. They were both surprised, and felt confused. They spoke first about the beauty of the morning. Then they spoke about the beauty of the garden. Sophia's smile was so sweet and her voice so soft that Tom said wildly: 'Oh, Miss Western. Can you wish me to die?'

'Indeed, Mr Jones,' she answered, looking down at the ground. 'I do not wish you any harm. But what do you mean?'

'What am I saying?' cried Tom. 'I have said too much. I would never offend you.'

'You do not offend me,' she said, 'but you surprise me.'

'My heart overflows,' said Tom. 'I struggle with my love and try to hide it, but it makes me ill. Soon I will die, and never trouble you again.'

Tom now started trembling, and Sophia felt faint.

'Mr Jones,' she said, weakly. 'I do understand you, but for heaven's sake, help me back into the house.'

Tom took her arm, and together they walked unsteadily back to the house without another word. Sophia went straight to her room. For Tom, there was unwelcome news.

Chapter 7 Mr Allworthy Falls Ill

Mr Allworthy was sick. This was the news that Tom received. How sick? The doctor said he was in very serious danger.

Mr Allworthy did not fear death. He now prepared himself calmly, and called his family to him. Everyone was there except his sister, Mrs Blifil, who was in London, and Tom, who rushed back from Mr Western's house immediately.

When the family and the servants were gathered around his bed, the good man spoke, but Blifil began to cry.

Taking Blifil's hand, Mr Allworthy said, 'Do not cry, my dear child. No one can escape death, and it does not matter when death comes. Life is like a party, which some leave early, and some leave later. There is little difference. Now, I wish to mention my will. Nephew Blifil, I leave you all my lands and property. To your mother I leave five hundred pounds a year, and the same amount to you, Mr Jones.'

Tom knelt beside the bed, took his godfather's hand and thanked him for his goodness both now and at all other times. 'Oh my friend! My father!' he said, then hot tears came into his eyes and he turned away.

'Mr Thwackum, I have given you a thousand pounds, and the same sum to you, Mr Square. I am sure this is more than you desire, but it is a sign of my friendship. My servants will share three thousand pounds. Now I find myself growing faint, so let me rest.'

Just then a servant came into the room and said there was a lawyer from London waiting downstairs with a message. Mr Allworthy sent Blifil to see him, and quietly fell asleep. Tom stayed in the room to watch over him.

Mr Thwackum and Mr Square left the room, looking unhappy. Perhaps they had expected more money. Blifil returned with a very sad face, and told them that his mother had died. 'You must bear this sad loss like a Christian,' advised Thwackum. 'Like a man,' said Square.

The doctor joined them, and they discussed whether to inform Mr Allworthy about the death of his sister. The doctor said no, but Blifil disagreed, so together they went to the sickroom to wake Mr Allworthy.

First the doctor checked the patient, and found him much better. Perhaps the danger was passing. Mr Allworthy opened his eyes, and heard the sad news from Blifil. He asked to see the lawyer, but Blifil said he had left in a great hurry to go somewhere else. Then Mr Allworthy asked Blifil to take care of his mother's funeral.

After dinner, when the doctor reported that the patient was now out of danger, Tom got wildly and happily drunk.

◆

Later, when Tom was still a little drunk, he decided to cool himself in the open air before returning to Mr Allworthy. It was a pleasant summer evening, made for love. Our hero walked beside a stream, thinking about his dear Sophia. Soon he threw himself on the ground and said: 'Oh Sophia. I will always love you, and you alone. If cruel Fortune separates us I will never love another.'

At these words he jumped up and saw – not his Sophia. No. Dressed in dirty clothes after a day's work in the fields, Molly Seagrim approached.

They started to speak, but I will not say what words. It is enough that they talked for a full quarter of an hour, and then disappeared among the trees.

Some of my readers might be surprised. But I suggest that Tom probably thought one woman better than none, and Molly probably imagined two men to be better than one.

Just then, Blifil and Mr Thwackum, who were taking a walk,

caught sight of the lovers as they disappeared.

'It's a man and a wicked woman,' cried Blifil.

They chased after the couple, making such a noise that Tom heard them. He leaped out from behind the trees.

'Is it you?' Thwackum said in a voice like thunder.

'Yes, it is me,' said Tom.

'And who is that wicked woman with you?'

'If I have any wicked woman with me, I will certainly not tell you who she is,' cried Tom.

'Then I must tell you plainly, I will discover her,' said Thwackum, moving forward.

'And I must tell you plainly, you will not,' said Tom.

With that, a great fight began. Blifil came forward to help, and Tom knocked him to the ground. Thwackum, who was a strong man and a champion fighter in his youth, attacked Tom furiously. Blifil got up again, and now the two together attacked our hero who, you may remember, was still weak from his broken arm.

Suddenly a fourth person joined in, shouting, 'Are you not ashamed to fight two against one?'

For a second time Tom knocked Blifil to the ground, and Thwackum attacked the newcomer, whom he now recognized. It was Mr Western. With his help, Tom won the day.

Mr Western's riding companions now arrived. They were the honest priest, Supple, Mrs Western, the aunt of Sophia, and the lovely Sophia herself. This is what they saw. In one place, Blifil lay on the ground, pale and breathless. Near him stood Tom, covered in blood. Some was his own, and some was once owned by Thwackum. Thwackum himself was there, looking bad-tempered. The last figure in the scene was Western the Great, standing proudly over everyone.

Everyone rushed to Blifil, who showed little sign of life. Then suddenly, a lovelier object lay lifeless on the ground. Sophia, perhaps at the sight of blood, had fainted.

Sophia opened her eyes and cried, 'Oh, heavens,' just as her father, her aunt and the priest rushed up.

Mrs Western saw her, and screamed. Immediately, two or three voices cried out, 'Miss Western is dead.'

Tom, who was trying to help Blifil, flew to Sophia, lifted her in his arms and ran over the field to the stream, where he threw water over her face, head and neck. Sophia opened her eyes and cried, 'Oh, heavens,' just as her father, her aunt and the priest rushed up.

This tragic scene now became a scene of joy. Mr Western kissed Sophia, and then Tom. There was nothing he would not give him, except his dogs and his two favourite horses.

Tom washed in the stream, and Sophia sighed when she saw the black and blue marks caused by Thwackum.

Then Western discovered the reason for the fight.

'What? Were you fighting for a woman?' he laughed. 'Where is she? Show me, Tom.' But Molly had crept away.

'Come gentlemen,' said Western. 'Be friends. Come home with me and make peace over a bottle.'

Thwackum and Blifil refused, but Tom and the priest followed Mr Western and his ladies home for an evening of joy and good humour.

Chapter 8 Mr Western Loses His Temper

It was Mrs Western, Sophia's aunt, who first noticed Sophia's behaviour. She spoke about it to her brother.

'Brother,' she said, 'have you not noticed something very extraordinary about my niece lately?'

'No, not I,' said Mr Western. 'Is there something the matter with my girl?'

'I think there is,' replied his sister.

'What is it then?' cried Western. 'Is she sick? Send for the best doctor, for I love her more than my own soul.'

27

Mrs Western smiled. 'There is no need for a doctor,' she said, 'for I believe Sophia is desperately in love.'

'What!' cried Western. 'In love without telling me? I'll punish her. I'll send her away, naked, without a penny!'

'You will not do that,' said his sister, 'until you know whether you approve of her choice. Perhaps the man she loves is exactly the man that you would choose for her.'

'That would make a difference,' agreed Western. 'If she loves the man I would choose she may love who she pleases.'

'That is spoken like a sensible man,' said his sister. 'Now what do you think of Mr Blifil? Did Sophia not faint when she saw him lying breathless on the ground?'

'By God,' said Western. 'You're right. And I am very pleased. I knew Sophy would not fall in love to make me angry. No one would be better than Blifil, for our two properties lie side by side as if they were married, and it would be a great pity to separate them. What should I do?'

'You should propose the marriage to Mr Allworthy.'

◆

Sophia had noticed that her aunt was watching her, so when her father invited Mr Allworthy and his family to dinner, she tried to hide her secret. She was very charming to Blifil, and paid no attention at all to poor Tom. Her aunt saw this as more evidence that Sophia loved Blifil.

After dinner, Mr Western took Mr Allworthy to one side and made his proposal. Mr Allworthy said that if the young people liked each other, he would be happy to agree. This attitude suprised Mr Western. He said that parents were the best judges, and he expected Sophia to be obedient. Mr Allworthy promised to discuss the matter with Blifil.

When they returned home, he told Blifil about Mr Western's proposal. After a short silence, Blifil told his uncle that he had not thought of marriage yet, but that he was glad to do what Mr Allworthy wanted. Mr Allworthy thought this answer was rather cold, but he wrote to Mr Western to say that his nephew had thankfully and gladly received the proposal, and was ready to visit the lady.

◆

Mr Western was very pleased with Mr Allworthy's message and replied immediately, inviting Mr Blifil to visit Sophia that very afternoon. He then asked his sister to tell her. Sophia was reading when her aunt came into her room.

'Is it a book about love?' asked Mrs Western, as Sophia put down her book. 'Ah, child, your cheeks are quite pink. Do you think I don't know the reason? Do you think the secret that you keep from your father can be kept from me? Come, you need not be ashamed.'

'But, madam,' said Sophia, looking a little foolish. 'Why should I be ashamed? What secret do you mean?'

'A secret which I saw plainly yesterday. Come, I am your friend. Tell me yourself, and I will give you happy news.'

'I know not what to say, madam,' said Sophia.

'I tell you child,' answered her aunt. 'We know your heart, and we entirely approve. This very afternoon your father has arranged for you to see your lover.'

'My father, this afternoon!' cried Sophia, turning pale.

'Yes, child,' said her aunt. 'This afternoon. And you have me to thank. I saw that you were in love when you fainted in the field, and I saw it again at supper. I know about these things, child. As soon as I told my brother he proposed the marriage to Mr Allworthy. Allworthy agreed, and your lover will come this afternoon.'

'This afternoon!' said Sophia. 'Dear aunt, you scare me!'

'Why, child? He's a charming young fellow.'

'It's true,' said Sophia. 'He is perfect. So brave, and yet so gentle. So kind, so clever, and so handsome. What does it matter that he is poor?'

'Poor! What do you mean? Mr Blifil, poor!'

Sophia turned pale and said faintly, 'Mr Blifil?'

'Yes, Mr Blifil. Who else have we been talking about?'

'Good heavens,' said Sophia. 'I thought of Mr Jones.'

'I protest,' cried her aunt. 'Now *you* scare *me*. Is it Mr Jones, and not Mr Blifil, who is the object of your love?'

'Mr Blifil!' repeated Sophia. 'Can you possibly be serious? If so, I am the unhappiest woman in the world.'

Mrs Western stood silent for a few minutes while fire filled her eyes. Then, in a voice of thunder, she said, 'And can you possibly think of disgracing your family by marrying a bastard? Can the blood of the Westerns be destroyed? Are you not ashamed to admit this to my face?'

Sophia was shaking. 'Madam,' she said, 'what I have said, you forced me to say. I never planned to tell anyone, but to take my secret thoughts with me to my grave.'

Sophia began to cry, but Mrs Western was not moved. She continued to show her anger for a full quarter of an hour. Then she threatened to go immediately to tell her brother.

Sophia threw herself at her aunt's feet and begged her to keep her secret, for fear of her father's temper. At last her aunt agreed, on one condition: Sophia must receive Mr Blifil that afternoon as the man who was to be her husband.

Sophia promised, but begged her aunt to help her delay the marriage. She hoped her father would change his mind when he knew how much she disliked Mr Blifil.

'No, no, Sophy,' said Mrs Western. 'To protect you from dishonour there is not a moment to lose. When you are a wife you may love whom you wish, but not before.'

◆

'Come, come, no tears,' said Mr Western that afternoon. 'Are you crying because I am going to marry you to the man you love? Your mother was the same, but she soon stopped after we were married. Mr Blifil will soon put an end to your tears. Cheer up, cheer up. He'll be here soon.'

Sophia kept her promise to her aunt. When Mr Blifil came, her father left them alone together. There was a very long silence, then some polite words, and then Sophia returned to her room. Mr Blifil was satisfied. He believed she was shy, like all young ladies on their first visit from a lover. He was confident that she admired him, and of course he had not the least idea about Tom.

When Blifil left, Mr Western went to find his Sophia. He told her, with kisses, that she was his only joy on earth. She must choose whatever clothes and jewels she pleased. He had no other use for his fortune than to make her happy. He was so loving that Sophia thought she would never have a better opportunity to tell him her feelings.

She thanked her father many times for his kindness, then fell to her knees. She begged him not to make her the most miserable thing on earth by forcing her to marry a man she hated. 'I ask you this, dear sir,' said she, 'since you are so very kind to tell me your happiness depends on mine.'

'What!' said Western, staring wildly.

'Oh, sir,' continued Sophia. 'I cannot live with Mr Blifil. To force me to marry him would be to kill me.'

'You can't live with Mr Blifil!' said Western.

'No sir, I can't,' answered Sophia.

'Then die, and to hell with you,' cried he.

'Can the best of fathers break my heart?' cried Sophia.

'Pooh! Pooh! Can marriage kill you? Nonsense!' cried he.

'Oh, sir,' answered she. 'Such a marriage is worse than death. I hate him more than I can say.'

'You will marry him,' shouted Western. 'And if you don't, I'll not give you a single penny. If I saw you starving in the street I would not give you a piece of bread!'

He then pushed her away so violently that her face hit the floor, and he burst out of the room.

Chapter 9   Blifil's Revenge

When Western flew into the hall he saw Tom, and told him what had happened. Tom was astonished, but offered to help.

'Go to her,' said the furious man. 'See what you can do.'

Tom went instantly to Sophia, and found her rising from the ground where her father had left her. She had tears in her eyes and blood on her lips.

'Oh, Mr Jones,' she cried, 'why did you save my life? My death would have made us both happier.'

'My heart bleeds, dearest Sophia,' said Tom. 'Your cruel father told me everything, and he himself sent me here.'

'He sent you? Surely you are dreaming,' answered Sophia.

'He sent me to persuade you to marry my hateful rival. Promise that you will never give yourself to Blifil.'

'That hateful name,' said she. 'I promise I will never give him what it is in my power to keep from him.'

'Now then,' cried Tom, 'please tell me that I may hope.'

'Hope for what?' said Sophia sadly. 'I do not care about my own ruin, but I cannot make my father miserable.'

The lovers stood in silence for a moment, her hand in his. Suddenly, the silence was broken by a terrible roar. Mrs Western had just told her brother Sophia's secret.

The idea of a marriage between Tom and his daughter had never once entered Mr Western's head. He believed equality in fortune was as necessary to a marriage as difference of sex. He thought his daughter could no more fall in love with a poor man as fall in love with an animal. He was therefore violently shocked by his sister's news.

Sophia turned pale at the terrible sound of her father's approach, and fainted in her lover's arms.

When Mr Western burst open the door and saw this, all his anger disappeared. He ran to his daughter, roaring for help. Soon servants, aunt and priest arrived with water and medicine, and Sophia was carried off by the women.

Now Mr Western turned to Tom, and his anger returned. If Mr Supple, who was a strong man, had not held him back, battle would have followed. Mr Western now swore and cursed like a country man at a dog fight. Very calmly, Tom said, 'Sir, I cannot lift my hand against the father of Sophia.'

These words made Mr Western curse and struggle even more, and Mr Supple begged Tom to leave. Tom thanked him for this advice, and immediately departed.

♦

The next morning, immediately after breakfast, Mr Western rode to Mr Allworthy's house and shouted at him.

'There, you really have done a fine piece of work!'

'What can be the matter, Mr Western?' said Allworthy.

'What's the matter? My daughter has fallen in love with your bastard, that's all. But I won't give her a penny. I always thought it was a bad thing to bring up a bastard like a gentleman and let him visit fine houses.'

'I am extremely sorry,' cried Allworthy.

'To hell with your sorrow, sir,' said Western. 'It will do me no good when I have lost my only child, my poor Sophy, who was the joy of my heart. But I will throw her out of the house. She will beg and starve in the streets.'

'But sir,' said Allworthy. 'Why did you give Tom so many

33

opportunities to be with her? Did you not see any signs?'

'Who could have known? The devil did not come to visit her – he came to hunt with me! I never saw them kiss once. But she *will* marry Mr Blifil, I promise you. Just keep your bastard away from my house. If I catch him, I'll kill him!'

Mr Western then rode back home to lock up his daughter.

Mr Blifil, who had watched this scene in silence, now said to his uncle, 'I am sorry, sir, that Mr Jones has once again upset you. If you knew what I knew about him . . .'

'What? Do you know anything worse than I already know?'

This was Blifil's opportunity to get revenge on Tom.

'The very day your life was in danger,' he began, 'when myself and all your family were in tears, Mr Jones drank and sang and roared with happiness, and then he beat me.'

'What?' cried Allworthy. 'Did he dare to strike you?'

'He did,' replied Blifil. 'That very evening, Mr Thwackum and I were walking in the fields, and we saw him lying with a woman. When we spoke to him, Jones struck me down, and beat Mr Thwackum too.'

'Oh, child,' said his uncle. 'In your goodness you have kept silent about this too long.'

Mr Allworthy first called for Mr Thwackum, who showed him the black and blue marks that still remained on his chest. Then he spent some hours alone, deciding how to punish Tom.

The poor young man came in to dinner as usual, but his heart was so heavy that he could not eat. After dinner, Mr Allworthy spoke to him for a long time. He reminded Tom of all the bad things he had done in the past, and told him what he had heard from Blifil. He ended by saying that if these recent things were true, Tom must leave for ever.

Poor Tom could not defend himself, as Blifil's story was partly true. His heart was almost broken already, and his spirits were so low that he could deny nothing. He asked Mr Allworthy to forgive him, and hoped he did not deserve the greatest punishment in the world.

Mr Allworthy answered that he had forgiven Tom too often, gave him an envelope and said goodbye. Though the envelope contained five hundred pounds, the gossips afterwards said that Tom was sent away penniless, and even naked, by his cruel father.

♦

Tom was told to leave the house immediately. He could send for his clothes later. And so he walked away in a dream.

After about a mile he stopped to rest by a little stream. His angry thoughts flew in many directions, and it was some time before he was cool enough to consider what to do next.

First, he decided to write to Sophia. The thought of leaving her nearly broke his heart, but he could not ruin her. He emptied his pockets to find paper, and he wrote:

Madam, I must fly for ever from your dear sight. When you hear of my hard fortune, do not be concerned. After losing you, nothing else is important. Oh, my Sophia! It is hard to leave you. Please forget me. May angels protect you.

Then he walked away, wondering how to send the letter. After some time he realized that his pockets were empty. He had left everything beside the stream. He hurried back.

On the way he met his old friend, the gamekeeper. They returned to the stream together to look for Tom's things. They looked everywhere but found nothing. This was not surprising, as they did not look in the gamekeeper's pockets. Black George was a dishonest fellow, and did not mention that he had found Tom's things earlier.

At last Tom gave up hope of finding his belongings. He decided to forget them, even Mr Allworthy's envelope, which he had never opened. He then asked George to take his letter to

Sophia's house and give it to her maid. George did this gladly, and returned with this letter for Tom.

Sir, as you know my father's temper, please avoid him. I wish I could send you more comfort, but believe this: nothing will make me give my hand or heart to another.

Tom kissed the letter a hundred times, but as it did not change his situation, he said goodbye to George and set off for the nearest town.

Chapter 10 Sophia Makes a Decision

Tom slept that night at an inn, and sent for his clothes. They arrived next morning with a letter from Blifil, which advised him to change his life, with the help of God. It also repeated Mr Allworthy's wish for Tom to leave for ever. This caused a flood of tears, but soon they dried.

'I must obey Mr Allworthy,' Tom decided. 'I will go this moment. But where? And what can I do without money?'

He decided to go to sea. But before we follow him we must return to see what has happened to the charming Sophia.

♦

The morning that Mr Jones left, Mr Western allowed his sister to unlock Sophia's door.

'I have promised your father,' said Mrs Western, 'to make you agree to marry Mr Blifil. What is your objection?'

'A very solid one, madam,' said Sophia. 'I hate him.'

'Sophy,' said her aunt. 'In the world it is out of fashion, romantic nonsense to want to like your husband.'

'But I will not marry Blifil,' said Sophia.

Western, who was listening outside, then entered the room

shouting, 'You, sister, have taught her to be disobedient! She was very obedient when she was a little child, before you took her away to teach her the ways of the world!'

'I, brother? I? It is you, with your terrible country ways, who have destroyed all my good teaching.'

Brother and sister then had a loud argument, until Mrs Western angrily called her carriage and left his house.

'Sir,' cried Sophia, 'I am sure your sister loves you. She has left you her whole fortune in her will.'

These words shocked Western. Might his sister now change her will? He hurried after her carriage to apologize.

They returned together, and Mrs Western now suggested that the marriage take place as soon as possible.

Blifil was invited to visit Sophia again the next day.

'Go to her, boy,' cried Western. 'Allworthy and I can finish the agreement today. You can marry her tomorrow!'

Blifil did not object. Sophia's tears brightened her eyes, and her breasts rose higher with her sighs. His desire for her was mixed with pleasure at defeating his hated rival, but most of all he wanted Sophia's wealth. So Blifil pretended to love her, and said that she loved him.

When the agreement was signed and the lawyers had left, Sophia's maid came running to see her.

'Dear madam,' said Mrs Honour, 'do not be shocked at what I have to tell you. Just now I heard my master telling Mr Supple to get a licence for you to be married tomorrow!'

'Honour,' said Sophia. 'I am shocked. What can I do?'

'Well, madam. If I was in your place I would not find it difficult, for Mr Blifil is a charming, sweet man.'

'Honour, I would kill myself first,' said Sophia.

'Oh, madam, don't frighten me with such wicked thoughts.'

'Honour,' continued Sophia, 'I know what I must do. I must leave my father's house this very night, and if you are my

'Go to her, boy,' cried Western. 'Allworthy and I can finish the
agreement today. You can marry her tomorrow!'

friend, you will keep me company.'

'I will, madam, to the world's end,' answered Honour. 'But where can you possibly go?'

'To London,' said Sophia. 'I know a lady of quality there who is a distant relation of mine. I met her when I was staying with my aunt, and she often invited me to visit her. So we will go to London.'

◆

We left Tom on the road to Bristol, planning to seek his fortune at sea. When it was almost dark, he stopped at an inn for dinner, and slept a while in a chair by the fire.

In the middle of the night there was a great thundering at the gate, and when the landlord opened it the kitchen was immediately full of soldiers in red coats, all calling for beer.

Tom woke up and enjoyed their company. When it was time for the soldiers to move on, they began to argue loudly about the bill. Tom stopped the argument by offering to pay. The men gave him a cheer and invited him to join them.

The redcoats were fighting for King George. They were marching against a rebel army from the north. Tom supported their cause, and said he would go with his new friends.

They marched for a day, with much joking and laughing, and in the evening they arrived at a place where an old captain was waiting for them. The captain was surprised to see that Tom was dressed like a gentleman. He invited Tom to dinner with himself and the rest of the officers.

After dinner, they talked about the war. One of the officers, called Northerton, was drunk. He took a dislike to Tom, and waited for a chance to make him look foolish.

The men decided to drink to the health of their ladies. When it was Tom's turn, he named Miss Sophia Western. He could not imagine that anybody present knew her.

'I knew a Sophy Western,' said Northerton. 'She went to bed

with half the young men of Bath. Is it the same woman?'

'Impossible,' said Tom. 'Miss Western is a young lady of great fashion and fortune.'

'Why, so she is,' said Northerton, who had seen Sophia walking in Bath with her aunt. He described her exactly, and added that her father had a great property in Somerset.

Tom did not really understand this kind of joke, so he turned to him and said, 'Please joke about something else.'

'Joke?' cried Northerton. 'I do not joke. Why, I remember that Tom French had both her and her aunt in bed!'

'Then I must tell you that you are a liar,' cried Tom.

Northerton cursed him and threw a bottle at his head. Tom fell to the ground and lay still. Northerton saw blood flowing from Tom's head, and decided it was time to leave, but the captain stopped him and asked, 'Was it true?'

'Not a bit,' said Northerton. 'I was just having a joke.'

'Then,' said the captain, 'as your joke has killed Mr Jones, you are my prisoner, sir, and deserve to be hanged.'

But Northerton broke away and escaped into the night.

Chapter 11 Tom Finds a Friend

Tom lay on the floor with no sign of life in him. The captain sent some soldiers to chase after Northerton, and then sent a servant to get a doctor.

Some officers picked up Tom's bloody body from the floor and put it in a chair. They saw that he still breathed, and began to argue about what to do. Soon the doctor arrived, and ordered his patient to be taken instantly to bed.

After seeing Tom, the doctor returned downstairs, where the captain was sitting with the landlady of the inn.

'Will he die?' asked the captain.

'We will all die, sir,' answered the doctor.

'But do you think he is in danger?' asked the landlady.

'I cannot say,' said the doctor.

'It's a terrible thing to spill human blood,' said the landlady, 'except when it is the blood of our enemies. I hope all our enemies are killed, for then the war will end and our taxes will be lower.'

Later that night, Tom woke and called for the captain. He said he felt much better, and told the captain he needed a sword, so that he could fight Mr Northerton.

'I love your brave spirit, my boy,' said the old captain, 'but after such a blow and so much loss of blood you are weak, and you must rest.'

'But what about my honour?' cried Tom.

'Your honour must wait, young gentleman,' said the captain, 'for I am afraid Mr Northerton has escaped.'

The captain left and Tom slept again. When he woke it was late in the afternoon, and he called for some tea. When the landlady brought it up she said that the doctor had gone and all the soldiers and officers had marched away. Tom asked her to prepare some food, and to send him a barber.

He felt in perfect health and spirits. While he was waiting for the barber he chose some clean clothes to wear.

The barber soon arrived with soap and hot water and began to shave Tom very slowly. Tom asked him to hurry.

'I never hurry,' said the barber. '*Festina lente*, I say.'

'You speak Latin,' said Tom. 'You are a man of learning!'

'A poor one, sir,' said the barber. 'Indeed, learning has ruined me. My father wanted me to be a dancing teacher but instead of learning to dance I learned to read Latin. He hated me for that, and left all his money to my brothers.'

'I would like to get to know you better,' said Tom. 'Will you do me the honour of drinking a glass with me tonight?'

'Sir, I will do you twenty honours, if you wish.'

'How can you do that, my friend?'

'Why, I will drink a whole bottle with you, if you wish, for you are a good man and I love a good conversation.'

Jones now walked downstairs neatly dressed, looking so handsome that one of the servant girls fell violently in love with him in five minutes. While he ate his dinner, the barber sat in the kitchen with the landlady.

'He is no young gentleman,' she told the barber. 'I have heard he was turned away from Mr Allworthy's house.'

'A servant, then?' said the barber. 'What's his name?'

'Jones, he told me, but perhaps he uses a false name.'

'If his name is Jones, he told you the truth,' said the barber, strangely, 'and perhaps he is Mr Allworthy's son.'

After dinner, Tom called for a bottle and the barber joined him. Tom poured out a glass of wine and raised it.

'To your good health, *doctissime tonsorum*,' he said.

'*Ago tibi gratias, domine*,' replied the barber. Then he asked, 'Sir, is it possible that your name is Jones?'

'It is,' said Tom.

'How strange,' said the barber. 'Mr Jones, you don't know me, which is not surprising as you only saw me once when you were very young. How is the good Mr Allworthy?'

'You seem to know me,' said Tom, a little suspiciously.

'May I ask, sir, why you are travelling this way?'

'Fill the glass, Mr Barber, and ask no more questions.'

'I apologize, sir. When a gentleman like you travels without servants we may suppose he is *in casu incognito*. But I promise you I can keep a secret.'

'That is unusual in your profession, Mr Barber.'

'Ah, sir,' answered the barber. 'I was not always a barber. *Non si male nunc et olim sic erit*. I have spent most of my life among gentlemen. I have a great respect for you. People talked about the good nature you showed to Black George, and they loved you for it. I am your friend.'

Every miserable man needs a friend, and Tom was not only miserable, he was also open-hearted. The barber's behaviour and his bits of poor Latin suggested that he was no ordinary fellow. So Tom told him why he was going to sea.

The barber noticed that there was one thing that Tom left out of his story. Though he said that he was Blifil's rival in love, he carefully avoided naming the young lady concerned. When the barber asked him, Tom paused a moment, then said, 'I trust you, ·sir. Her name is Sophia Western.'

'Mr Western's daughter is now a woman!' cried the barber. 'I remember her father as a boy. Well, *tempus edax rerum*.'

Tom was tired now, and went up to his room to rest. In the morning he sent for the doctor, but he was not to be found, and the barber was called instead.

Tom was surprised. 'I asked for the doctor, Mr Barber,' he said. 'I want him to open my bandage.'

'Well, sir,' replied the barber. 'I am also a doctor, and if you wish me to open your bandage I am willing.'

Though Tom was not very confident, the man seemed serious, so he allowed him to open the bandage and look at his head. When the barber saw Tom's wound he made shocked noises.

Tom suspected he was joking. 'Stop playing the fool,' he said, angrily. 'What is your opinion? Answer seriously!'

'Why, then,' cried the other, 'if I may put on a clean bandage, I promise you will soon be well.'

'Well, Mr Barber, or Mr Doctor, or Mr Barber-Doctor,' said Tom, as the new bandage was applied. 'You are one of the strangest men I ever met. There must be something very surprising in your story. I would like to hear it.'

'You shall hear it,' said his friend. 'But first let me lock the door so that we are not interrupted.' He did so, and then said, 'I must begin, sir, by telling you that you have been my greatest enemy.'

'I, your enemy?' said Tom, amazed.

'Please don't be angry, sir, for you were just a baby and did not mean to harm me. I think you will understand everything when I tell you my name. Have you ever heard, sir, the name of Partridge? A man who was honoured to be called your father, and who was ruined by that honour?'

'I have heard that name,' said Tom, 'and I have always believed that I am that man's son.'

'Well, sir, I am Partridge, but you are not my son!'

Chapter 12 An Angel Appears to a Woman in Trouble

Partridge was sure that this extraordinary meeting with the person who caused all his bad fortune was a sign that good fortune was coming, so he was determined to follow Tom.

Tom said he would do everything in his power to help the unfortunate man. 'But,' he added, 'perhaps you think I will be able to pay you, Mr Partridge, but really I cannot.' And he showed Partridge his purse.

Now Partridge firmly believed that Tom was Mr Allworthy's son, and he could not imagine why that good man would send his son away. He therefore believed that Tom had made up the story, and that he was actually running away from his father. If Partridge could persuade Tom to return to his father, Mr Allworthy would certainly reward him well.

He said to Tom, 'I see you have very little money now, sir, but things will change in the future. I am not asking for payment. Just let me travel with you as your friend.'

And so, taking a few clean shirts and leaving the rest of Tom's things locked up in Partridge's house, they set off.

♦

Tom was very pleased with Partridge's company, and the two walked along together until they came to Gloucester. Here, they ate dinner in an inn, and then Tom decided to continue walking through the night.

The clock struck five as the pair left Gloucester. As it was the middle of winter, it was dark, but a bright moon gave them light. Tom remembered some romantic poems about the moon, Partridge added some comments in Latin, and they travelled on for about five miles in this way.

Suddenly, Tom stopped and said, 'Who knows, Partridge? The loveliest lady in all the world may be looking at that moon this very moment.'

'Perhaps, sir,' said Partridge. 'But if you wish to have your lady in your arms again, why don't we go back now?'

'If you wish to go back,' said Tom, 'I will thank you and give you some money, but I am determined to go on.'

'Then I am determined to follow you,' said Partridge.

They walked on through the cold night, and when the sun came up they found a place on a hill to sleep. Tom was the first to wake. From a wood below the hill came a woman's violent screams. Tom listened for a moment, then ran down the hill and into the wood.

There he saw a shocking sight. A woman, half naked, with a belt around her neck, and a man who was trying to hang her from a tree.

Tom asked no questions, but took his stick and beat the man to the ground. He continued beating him until the woman begged him to stop.

The poor thing then fell to her knees and thanked him. As he lifted her up she said, 'You must be a good angel.'

Indeed he was a charming figure, and if an angel has youth, health, strength, freshness, spirit and good nature, then Tom certainly looked like one.

The woman looked less like an angel. She was middle-aged, and not much of a beauty, but in her torn clothes she looked very attractive to Tom. They stood in silence until the man on the ground began to move. Looking at his face, Tom was greatly surprised to see that it was Mr Northerton.

Tom took Northerton's belt and tied his hands behind him. Then he helped him to his feet, saying, 'Northerton, do you remember me? You insulted me and nearly killed me. Fortune has brought us together again for me to punish you.'

Tom asked the woman where she could get some clothes, but she said she was a stranger in that part of the country. Tom then told them both to wait while he looked for help.

When he returned, unsuccessful, the woman was alone. Though Northerton's hands were tied, his feet were free, and he had walked off through the wood.

'Do not spend time looking for him,' begged the woman. 'Please take me to the nearest town.'

Jones offered her his coat to cover herself with, but for some reason she absolutely refused it. 'Then I will walk in front of you, and will not offend you by looking back,' said Tom. And though he did try to keep looking ahead, the lady often asked him to turn around to help her. And so our hero brought his companion safely into the town of Upton.

◆

When they arrived, Tom took the lady to the best inn in the street, and asked for a room upstairs. As they followed a servant up to the room, the landlord shouted, 'Hey, where is that beggar woman going? Come downstairs!'

'Leave the lady alone,' cried Tom from above. Then, leaving his companion in her room, he returned downstairs to ask the landlady to send her up some clothes.

Now the inn at which our travellers had arrived was very

respectable. Good ladies from Ireland and the north of England liked to stay there on their way to Bath. While the landlady could not expect every conversation that took place under her roof to be perfectly innocent, she did not want the inn to get a bad name. Tom and his half-naked companion must go before they harmed her reputation.

The landlady had picked up a heavy kitchen pot and was just about to go upstairs when Tom came in, asking for some clothes. As they stood there, the landlord arrived, calling the lady upstairs all the bad names he could think of.

Tom hit the landlord, the landlady lifted her pot to hit Tom, and at this moment Partridge walked in, glad to find Tom again. Seeing the danger, Partridge caught hold of the landlady's arm. She turned and knocked him to the ground.

The sound of a carriage and horses outside put a sudden stop to this bloody war. The landlord and his wife rushed out to meet the new guests. A young lady and her maid had arrived, and were taken upstairs to the best room.

Tom rushed to pick up faithful Partridge from the floor, and sent him outside to wash his bloody nose at the water pump. Now the naked lady came down, asking about all the noise. She found a tablecloth to cover herself with.

At this moment, a soldier arrived, demanding beer and somewhere to sleep. He noticed Tom's lady companion.

'Madam,' said the soldier in surprise. 'Are you not Captain Waters's lady? Have you had some kind of accident?'

'I have indeed,' said Mrs Waters, 'and I have to thank this gentleman for rescuing me.'

'Whatever this gentleman has done, my lady,' said the soldier, 'I am sure the captain will thank him for it. And if I can help you, please command me.'

Hearing these words, the landlady now rushed into the kitchen, apologizing to Mrs Waters for her behaviour and offering her some clothes to wear. 'How could I know that a fashionable lady like you would appear in such rags?' she cried. 'If I had suspected that my lady was my lady, I would have burned my tongue out before I said what I said.'

Tom begged Mrs Waters to forgive the landlady and to accept her clothes, and the two women went upstairs. Partridge soon came back, the landlord brought in beer and perfect calm returned to the kitchen.

Chapter 13 An Inn's Reputation is Put at Risk

Tom had not eaten for twenty-four hours, so when Mrs Waters invited him to have dinner with her in her room, he was happy to accept. While three pounds of meat which were once part of an animal now became part of Tom, Mrs Waters watched him with other things on her mind.

Now Tom was really one of the handsomest young men in the world. His face was the picture of health, with signs of sweetness and good nature which were noticed by everyone who saw him. He was strong, active, gentle and good-tempered, and people enjoyed his cheerful company.

Mrs Waters saw all this, and formed a very good opinion of him. In fact she had fallen in love with Tom, and she wanted him to know it. How could she show him?

First she shot sharp looks from her two lovely blue eyes, but these only hit a piece of meat which Tom was then putting on his plate. Then a heavy sigh lifted her fair breasts, but its sweet sound was lost as he opened a bottle of beer. Many other tricks were tried, but while our hero was eating, hunger defended him against love.

When dinner was over, the attack began again with a smile which showed more than just pretty white teeth. This smile our

Mrs Waters had fallen in love with Tom, and she wanted him to know it.

hero received with full force, and he began to see the enemy's plan. He defended himself weakly, trying to think about his fair Sophia. But his heart was soon captured by Mrs Waters, and we will now politely leave the room.

♦

Meanwhile, the couple upstairs were the topic of conversation in the kitchen, where the landlord sat with his wife, Partridge, the soldier and the carriage driver.

The soldier explained that Mrs Waters was the wife of a captain, though some people said they were not actually married. People also said she was a good friend of Mr Northerton's, though the captain knew nothing about that.

The soldier then asked where Partridge and his master were travelling. 'He's not my master,' said Partridge. 'We are friends. *Amicum sumus*. I am a schoolteacher, and he is one of the greatest gentlemen in the country.'

'Then why does such a great gentleman walk about the country on foot?' asked the landlord.

'I really don't know,' answered Partridge. 'He has a dozen horses and servants in Gloucester, but last night he decided to walk.'

The soldier then began to drink to the king, and after a while he suggested a fight. The carriage driver agreed to fight for a bet, and the two took off their shirts and fought each other fiercely, until the soldier won.

The young lady who had been resting upstairs now sent down orders for her carriage to be prepared, as she was ready to continue her journey. Impossible. To speak plainly, the carriage driver was now completely drunk. So was the soldier. Partridge was not much better.

The landlady was called to take tea upstairs to Mr Jones and Mrs Waters, and she told them this news. 'She is such a sweet, 'pretty lady,' she said, 'and in such a hurry to leave. I am sure she is in love and running away to meet a young gentleman.'

At these words, Tom sighed heavily. Mrs Waters noticed. She suspected she might have a rival, but she did not mind. Tom's beauty charmed her eyes, but because she could not see his heart she did not worry about it.

Nor did she bother to tell him about her own situation. Though Tom was careful not to ask her questions which might embarrass her, the reader will surely want to know. So, here are the real facts.

This lady had lived for some years with Captain Waters, pretending to be his wife and using his name. I am sorry to say she was also very friendly with Mr Northerton. It was a friendship that did her reputation no good.

When Northerton threw the bottle which hit Tom's head, he thought it had killed him. He escaped punishment by running off into the night, and it was to Mrs Waters that he ran.

Captain Waters was away at that time, so Mrs Waters agreed to help Northerton to get away to a seaport where he could escape abroad. She offered to walk with him to a place where he could get a horse, and she said she would give him some of her money.

Northerton noticed that she had ninety pounds in her purse and a diamond ring on her finger, and he made another plan. When they reached a lonely wood, he suddenly took off his belt, grabbed the poor woman and tried to kill her. It was at this moment that our hero had arrived to rescue her.

♦

It was now midnight, and everyone was in bed except Susan, the kitchen maid, who was washing the kitchen floor. Suddenly, a gentleman on horseback arrived, and rushed into the kitchen to ask if there was a lady in the inn. The late hour and his wild behaviour surprised Susan, but when the gentleman said he was looking for his wife she immediately thought he was Mr Waters. She accepted some money from the gentleman, and took him upstairs to Mrs Waters's room.

In the polite world, a gentleman always knocks before he enters his wife's bedroom. This gentleman did knock, but in such a violent way that the door flew open and he fell into the room. As he got to his feet again he saw (we admit it with shame and sorrow) our hero himself in bed, demanding to know the reason for this rude behaviour.

The gentleman was about to apologize when he saw, in the moonlight, various pieces of a woman's clothing on the floor. In a jealous rage, he rushed to the bed.

Tom jumped out of the bed to stop him. And now Mrs Waters (for we must confess she was in the same bed) began to scream, 'Murder! Robbery!' until the guest in the next room rushed in to help.

This guest was an Irishman who was on his way to Bath. He stood at the door, holding a candle in one hand and his sword in the other. He looked at the furious gentleman and cried out, 'Mr Fitzpatrick, what is the meaning of this?'

The gentleman immediately answered, 'Oh, Mr Maclachlan, I am glad you are here. This devil is in bed with my wife!'

'Your wife?' cried Mr Maclachlan. 'I know Mrs Fitzpatrick very well, and I don't see her here.'

Fitzpatrick now looked more closely at the lady in the bed and saw his unfortunate mistake. He began to apologize.

At that moment, the landlady came in, and Mrs Waters quickly called out to her, 'What kind of place is this? All these men have broken into my room to rob me!'

Fitzpatrick, hanging down his head, explained his mistake, apologized again and left with his friend. Tom explained that he had rushed in to help Mrs Waters when he heard all the noise. 'Thank God my reputation is not ruined,' cried the landlady.

'There has never been a robbery in my inn. Only good, honest people come here.' And she returned downstairs.

And what about Mr Fitzpatrick? After he had disturbed the house in this unfortunate way, the reader will find it hard to believe he was a gentleman.

Mr Fitzpatrick was indeed born a gentleman, but without any money. Luckily, he had married a young woman with a fortune. He was cruel to his wife, but generous with her fortune. Now he had spent it all, and she had run away.

Mr Fitzpatrick had followed his wife, and was sure he would find her in the inn at Upton. After his terrible mistake, he never thought she might be in another room. Tired and disappointed, he accepted Mr Maclachlan's kind offer to share his bed for the rest of the night.

Chapter 14 The Ring on His Pillow

The landlady went downstairs to talk to Susan about the night's events, and Partridge, who was always looking for a chance to drink and talk, joined them in the kitchen.

After a while, two new people arrived at the inn, two young women in riding clothes. One of them was so richly dressed that Partridge crept into a corner to admire her.

The lady in the rich clothes asked if she could warm herself at the kitchen fire. She didn't want to eat, and said they could only stay an hour or two because they were in a hurry. The landlady sent Susan upstairs to light a fire in a bedroom where the lady could rest.

When the lady was settled in the bedroom, her hungry maid came back downstairs to the kitchen and ordered a chicken.

Now the chicken was still alive, and the maid was hungry. The landlady suggested other meat, but the maid was as delicate as a queen about her food. 'Indeed,' she said, 'I believe this is the first time I have ever sat in a kitchen to eat. I am glad there are no poor people here. You, sir, look like a gentleman.'

'Yes, yes, madam,' cried Partridge, 'I am a gentleman. I am here with the son of great Mr Allworthy of Somerset.'

'I know Mr Allworthy very well,' said the maid. 'And I know that he has no son alive.'

This confused Partridge a little, but he answered, 'Well, madam, not everybody knows this, for Mr Allworthy was never married to the mother, but Mr Jones is certainly his son.'

'You surprise me, sir,' cried the maid. 'Mr Jones is in this inn?' And she rushed upstairs.

Sophia (for this was the richly dressed young lady) was resting with her lovely head on her hand when her maid entered the room crying, 'Madam, who do you think is here?'

Sophia sat up and cried, 'Not my father!'

'No, madam,' said Honour, the maid. 'It is Mr Jones!'

Sophia sent Honour back to the kitchen to ask Mr Jones's friend to wake him immediately.

Partridge refused. 'My friend went to bed very late.'

'I promise he will not be angry,' Honour insisted.

'Another time,' answered Partridge. 'One woman at a time is enough for any reasonable man.' He then told Honour directly, for he was more than a little drunk, that Jones was in bed with another woman.

When Honour told Sophia this, she did not believe it. At that moment Susan came in to check the fire. Sophia asked her what she knew, and, with the help of some money from Sophia, the story came out. Then Susan said, 'If you like, madam, I can creep into the young man's room and see if he is in his own bed.' Sophia agreed, so she did this, and came back to say that Tom's bed was empty.

Then Susan said that Mr Jones had told everybody about

Sophia. 'He told us, madam, that you were dying of love for him, but he was going to the war to get rid of you. But how could he leave such a fine, rich, beautiful lady as you to be with another man's wife?'

Sophia sent Susan downstairs to order the horses. Then she burst into tears. After some time, she thought of a way to punish Tom. She gave Honour her favourite ring, and asked her to leave it on the pillow in Tom's empty room. She then paid her bill and rode away with her maid.

♦

It was now past five in the morning. During the night, the other young lady, deciding not to wait for her carriage driver, had left the inn on horseback with her maid.

Other people were now waking up. Tom returned to his room to get dressed, and called Partridge.

'Oh, sir,' cried Partridge. 'Why should any man go to these *horrida bella*, these bloody wars, when he can go home and have everything he needs?'

'Partridge, you are a coward,' cried Tom. 'You may go home if you wish, but I will not.'

'Then I will stay,' said Partridge, 'for you need me. Why, last night I protected you from two wicked women. And see, one of them was in your room, for there is her ring.'

'Oh, heavens, it is Sophia's,' cried Tom. 'Is she here?'

'She was, sir,' said a frightened Partridge, 'but by now she will be many miles away.'

'Then we will leave immediately,' cried Tom.

Downstairs, Mr Fitzpatrick and his friend Mr Maclachlan were making arrangements for a carriage to take them to Bath. At that moment, shouting loudly, a man arrived on horseback with several companions. It was Sophia's father.

Mr Western was asking loud questions about his daughter

when Tom came downstairs with Sophia's ring in his hand.

'My daughter's ring,' shouted Western. 'Where is she?'

'It is her ring,' said Tom. 'But I have not seen her.'

'He is a liar,' cried Mr Fitzpatrick, 'for I caught him in bed with her, and, sir, I'll take you to her room.'

Mr Western and Mr Fitzpatrick rushed up the stairs together, and once again Mrs Waters was disturbed by men bursting into her room. Mr Western was shocked, apologized and rushed off to look for Sophia in the other rooms. Mrs Waters now got dressed and prepared to leave.

When it was clear that there were no young ladies in the inn, Mr Western cursed everybody, ordered his horses and rode off with his companions. Mr Fitzpatrick invited Mrs Waters to travel to Bath in his carriage. Tom paid his bill and set off on foot with Mr Partridge. And that was the end of Tom's adventures at Upton.

Chapter 15 Sophia Finds a Place to Stay

When Sophia and Honour left Upton they asked their guide to travel towards London. They had just crossed a river when they heard the sound of horses behind them. Sophia ordered the guide to travel faster. Faster still came the horses behind them, and soon they were overtaken.

The travellers who joined Sophia were also a lady, her maid and a guide. Very politely, the two parties agreed to travel together. They rode steadily, without speaking, until daylight came. Then the two ladies, who were riding side by side, looked at each other and said with one breath: 'Sophia!' 'Harriet!'

The wise reader will not be surprised to learn that the lady whom Sophia recognized was Mrs Fitzpatrick, for she had indeed been staying in the inn they had just left. What will surprise you is that Harriet Fitzpatrick was Sophia's cousin. They had once lived together with their aunt, Mrs Western, and were dear friends until Harriet had run away to marry Mr Fitzpatrick at the age of eighteen.

In the afternoon they stopped at an inn to eat and rest. Sophia, who had not been to bed for two nights, slept until after the sun went down. When she woke, she ordered tea and told Harriet that she was travelling to London. Her cousin agreed to accompany her. She had planned to go to Bath, or to stay with her aunt Western, but her husband's sudden arrival at the inn in Upton had changed her mind.

Sophia now felt so fresh that she suggested leaving immediately. It was a clear night, and not too cold. Harriet begged her to wait until morning, so the two cousins stayed the night in the inn and exchanged stories.

Harriet's story was so tragic that when dinner came, Sophia could hardly eat. Harriet had suffered from cruelty, jealousy and terrible unhappiness, but her appetite seemed excellent, and she stopped for a while to enjoy her meal. Then she finished her story.

'Mr Fitzpatrick wanted the last of my money. He never beat me, but he did lock me in my room. I had no pen, no paper, no books, just a servant to make my bed every day and bring me food. I was desperate, but by very good fortune (well, I will not tire you with the details) I managed to escape. I made my way to Dublin, took a boat to England and was travelling to Bath when I stopped at Upton. My husband overtook me there last night, but though I heard him, he did not find me.'

Sophia gave a sigh. It was now time to tell her story, which she did, and I hope the reader will excuse me for not repeating it. But I will say one thing. She never mentioned Tom from beginning to end. It was as if he didn't exist.

♦

The ladies and their maids now got into the lord's carriage and set off.

Very late that evening, an Irish lord arrived at the inn. Learning that Mrs Fitzpatrick was upstairs, he sent the landlord up with a message.

Harriet seemed very pleased to receive the message, and invited the lord to visit them immediately. He seemed to be a very special friend. He was a neighbour of Harriet's in Ireland, and in fact it was with his help that she had managed to escape from her husband. But for some reason she had not given this information to Sophia.

The lord seemed surprised that Harriet was not in Bath. He very politely offered to take the two ladies to London in his carriage. Harriet accepted instantly.

When the lord left, Harriet spoke warmly about him, and his love for his wife, saying she believed he was the most faithful husband she knew. Then it was time for sleep.

◆

Next morning, the ladies paid their guides, and it was then that Sophia discovered she had lost something. It was a banknote which her father had given her to buy her wedding clothes. She searched everywhere, but the note was not to be found, and she realized she must have dropped it on the road when she pulled a handkerchief from her pocket.

The ladies and their maids now got into the lord's carriage and set off, accompanied by many servants. They travelled ninety miles in two days, and on the second evening arrived in London.

They were taken to the lord's house. As his wife was not in town, Harriet absolutely refused his invitation to stay in the house, and lodgings were found for her.

Sophia spent one night with her cousin, but next day sent a note to Lady Bellaston, the relative she had met at her aunt's house. She was immediately invited to stay with her.

Harriet seemed happy for Sophia to leave her alone, and

Sophia began to suspect the reason. She tried to give her cousin some wise advice. 'Consider what a dangerous situation you are in, my dear. You are a married woman, and your friend's wife is not here. People will gossip.'

Harriet was amused, and said, 'I will visit you soon, dear Sophy. Now, please try to forget your country ideas.'

So Sophia went to Lady Bellaston's house, where she found a warm welcome. Lady Bellaston promised to give her all the protection which it was in her power to give. And as we have now brought our heroine into safe hands, we can leave her there for a while and return to poor Tom.

Chapter 16 Rich Food

When Tom and his companion Partridge left Upton, they marched with heavy hearts, though for different reasons. They came to a crossroads, and Tom asked Partridge which road they should take. 'If you take my advice,' said Partridge, 'you will turn around and return home.'

'I have no home to return to,' cried Tom. 'Even if my godfather would take me back, I could not bear to live there without Sophia. Now, since I cannot follow her, let us follow the army. I believe they went this way.' And by chance Tom chose the road which Sophia had taken.

They marched on for several miles, and arrived at another crossroads. Here a poor man in rags asked them for money. Partridge was very rude to him, but Tom gave him a coin.

'Master,' cried the man, after thanking him. 'I have something interesting here, which I found about two miles away. As you are kind, I know you will not think I am a thief. Would you like to buy it?'

He then passed a little gold notebook to Tom. He opened it

and (guess, reader, what he felt) saw on the first page the words Sophia Western, written in her own fair hand. He kissed and kissed the page.

While he was kissing the book, as if he had a delicious little cake in his mouth, a piece of paper fell from its pages to the ground. Partridge picked it up and gave it to Tom, who shouted that it was a banknote for a hundred pounds.

Partridge was delighted at this news, and so was the honest man (though it is fair to say that perhaps he was honest because he could not read). Tom immediately told him that he knew the owner of the notebook, and would follow her and return it. He paid him a pound for the notebook, and asked him to lead them to the place where he found it.

They then walked together to the place where Sophia had unhappily dropped the notebook, and where the man had happily found it. Tom opened the notebook a hundred times, kissed it as often, and talked to himself as he walked.

When they arrived at the place, the poor man, who had been thinking about the banknote, now said to Tom: 'Please give me half the money I found.'

Tom refused. 'I will give it to the right owner,' he said. 'But let me write your name in the notebook and one day you may have a reward.'

Our travellers then left the man and moved on so fast that they had no breath for conversation. Tom thought about Sophia. Partridge thought about the banknote.

As they came into the next town they met three horses, led by a boy whom Partridge recognized as the guide who came to Upton with Sophia. The boy told Tom that Sophia did not need the horses any more, as she had continued her journey in a carriage. Tom quickly offered to pay him to take them to London instead. The boy agreed, and now Tom and Partridge continued their journey on horseback.

Reader, my pen will not describe the roads, the rivers and the other beauties which passed by as our travellers rode towards London. But one cold, wet night there was a conversation which I will repeat.

'Sir,' said Partridge. 'We have had no dinner today, yet you look fresh and strong. Do you live on love?'

'This dear notebook is my food,' said Tom. 'And very rich it is too.'

'Rich, yes,' cried Partridge, 'for it has enough in it to buy us a hundred dinners.'

'Partridge!' said Tom. 'What are you suggesting?'

'Oh, nothing dishonest,' answered Partridge. 'Where is the dishonesty in spending a little now, if you repay it later? As your own money is nearly finished, where can be the harm, if you need it? A great lady does not need it, especially if she is now with a lord.'

'Partridge,' said Tom firmly, 'finding and spending is the same as stealing, and stealing is a hanging matter. This note is the property of my own dear angel, and I will put it in no other hands but hers, even if I am starving.'

Chapter 17 Tom Receives an Invitation

When they arrived in London, Tom sent Partridge to find lodgings while he began his search for Sophia. He started looking for the house where the Irish lord lived. He walked through the streets until eleven that night, and began again early next morning. At last he found himself in the right street, and someone directed him to the lord's house.

Tom was dressed in country clothes, and these showed signs of many days on the road, so when he knocked on the door, the servant who opened it was not very polite. He said there were no ladies in the house, and that the lord was busy. Fortunately, another servant was listening. He followed Tom into the street and offered, for a sum of money, to show him where the two ladies were staying.

It was very bad luck that Tom arrived at Harriet's door about ten minutes after Sophia had left. The maid took a message upstairs, but Harriet sent back a message to say she was too busy to see Tom. He was sure that Sophia was in the house with her cousin, and probably angry about what had happened at Upton. He told the servant that he would call again in the evening, and spent all day in the street, watching the door, but nobody came out.

In the evening, he returned to Mrs Fitzpatrick's house. This time, she agreed to see him. Tom asked about Sophia, but Harriet told him nothing. She said that he could call again the following evening, then sent him away, as she was expecting another visitor. As nothing unusual happened during the next visit, which was from her friend, the Irish lord, we will pass quickly to the next morning.

Harriet worried about her cousin's unexpected visitor, and decided to ask the advice of Sophia's relative, Lady Bellaston. She got up before the sun, and at this unfashionable hour she went to Lady Bellaston's house, hoping to see her while Sophia was still in bed.

Lady Bellaston was very interested in Harriet's story. She especially liked her description of the young man: 'a very handsome fellow, and so charming'. Lady Bellaston thought she should see the fellow before deciding what to do. She promised to visit Harriet that evening, and told her to make sure Mr Jones was there.

◆

That winter's day was one of the shortest in the year, but to Tom it seemed one of the longest. Though six o'clock was the polite time to visit, it was soon after five when he knocked again on Harriet's door. She received him kindly, but still said she knew nothing about Sophia.

After some time, Tom decided to explain that he had a large sum of money that he wanted to deliver to Sophia. He showed Harriet the notebook and told her what it contained, and how it was found.

They were now interrupted by the arrival of an elegant lady, who was followed a little later by the Irish lord. Everyone bowed low to each other. Then a brilliant conversation began, which, though it was very fine, I shall not repeat. Tom watched this fashionable scene in polite silence, as nobody took any notice of him.

At last, Harriet asked Tom to tell her where she might find him the next day, and he soon left the company. Now the elegant visitors took a great deal of notice of him, but nothing they said was very kind, so I shall not repeat that either. Lady Bellaston then left. The lord, for some reason or other, now made Harriet promise she would not see Mr Jones again, and as nothing else passed between them of importance to us, we will return to our hero's affairs.

◆

The place where Tom had sent Partridge to find lodgings was a house in Bond Street where Mr Allworthy always stayed when he was in London. It was owned by Mrs Miller, a good woman whose husband had died, leaving her with two young daughters and not very much else. Though Tom did not know this, Mr Allworthy had given Mrs Miller the house and a sum of money for furniture, so that she could earn money by renting rooms.

Tom had a room on the second floor, and Partridge one on the fourth. On the first floor was a pleasant young gentleman called Mr Nightingale. When Tom arrived back that evening,

Nightingale invited him to share a bottle of wine.

Their friendly conversation was suddenly interrupted by a maid who brought in a packet which had been delivered by a stranger for Mr Jones. Inside was a mask, a ticket for a party the next evening and a message that said:

The Queen of Fairies sends you this. Be kind to her.

'You are a lucky man,' said Nightingale. 'I am sure these were sent by a lady who wants to meet you at the party.'

Tom did feel lucky. If Mrs Fitzpatrick had sent the packet, he might possibly see his Sophia at the party. He decided to go, and invited his new friend to go with him.

The next evening, Nightingale invited Tom to eat with him in town before the party, but Tom excused himself. To tell the truth, he had not a penny in his pocket, and had to borrow some coins from Partridge. Partridge took the opportunity to advise Tom, once again, to go home.

'How often must I tell you that I have no home to go to,' answered Tom. 'When Mr Allworthy gave me the envelope of money (I don't know how much it was, but I'm sure he was very generous) he said he never wanted to see me again.'

Partridge had never heard of this money before. He asked what had happened to it. Tom told him how he had left the envelope beside a stream in Somerset, and how he and Black George had gone back to look for it, but without success.

Then a message came saying that Mr Nightingale was back from dinner and was ready to leave for the party.

Chapter 18 Sophia Has a Rival

When the two men arrived at the party they walked about together for a while, then Mr Nightingale left Tom alone. As everyone was wearing masks, he looked for ladies with Sophia's shape and spoke to them, hoping they would answer with Sophia's voice, but none of them did.

Suddenly, a masked woman tapped him on the shoulder and said, 'Follow me.'

He followed her to the end of the room, where she sat down and said, in a soft voice, 'Miss Western is not here.'

'My good fairy queen,' said Tom. 'You have cleverly changed your voice, but I know you are Mrs Fitzpatrick. Please tell me where I might find Sophia.'

The mask answered, 'Do you think I would encourage my cousin in an affair which would end in her ruin? And did your fairy queen invite you here to speak about a rival?'

Tom realized that for this lady to bring him to Sophia, he must please her. So he began to be more charming. The two walked and talked for some time. To Tom's surprise, the lady greeted everyone by name, even though they wore masks.

'People of fashion,' she explained, 'know each other anywhere, and to them the masks are childish. You will see that they get bored quickly at this kind of party, and leave early. I myself am bored, and I believe you are too. I will leave now, and I hope you will not follow me. Indeed I won't know what to say if you do.'

From this, Tom realized that he should follow the lady, and he walked behind her carriage all the way to a house where the door opened to admit her and her follower.

Once inside, Tom begged her to take off her mask, and when at last she did, he discovered not Mrs Fitzpatrick but Lady Bellaston.

After that they had a very ordinary conversation, which, as it lasted from two until six o'clock in the morning, I shall not bore you with. The lady then promised to look for Sophia, and they agreed to meet again in the evening.

♦

Tom returned to his lodgings. After a few hours' sleep he called Partridge and showed him a banknote of fifty pounds, saying he could now repay his debt. Though Partridge was glad, he was also suspicious. As Tom was out all night, Partridge imagined his desperate master must have robbed someone. The reader must imagine the same, unless he suspects the generosity of Lady Bellaston.

In fact, the money was from the lady. Though she did not give much to hospitals and churches, she did think that young men without a penny in their pockets needed her help.

That evening, Mrs Miller came home from a visit to her cousin. The cousin was expecting a baby, her husband was out of work, her children were starving and the youngest was very sick. When he heard this sad story, Tom took Mrs Miller to one side and gave her his purse, asking her to spend as much as she needed to help these poor people. Mrs Miller was amazed, cried, took ten pounds, and said, 'I already know one kind man in the world. Now I know another.'

Mrs Miller then told Tom what Mr Allworthy had done for her when her husband died.

◆

That evening, Tom met Lady Bellaston again. They had another long conversation, but as it was just as ordinary as the one the previous evening, I shall not give details.

Tom grew more and more impatient to see Sophia, but if he mentioned her to Lady Bellaston, she became angry.

He was in a very uncomfortable situation. As Lady Bellaston had grown violently fond of him, he was now one of the best-dressed men about town. He believed her when she said that Sophia was deliberately hiding from him, and he could not forget that if ever they did come together, her father would never forgive her.

But even if he did not love Sophia, Tom could never love Lady Bellaston as her generosity deserved. She was in the autumn of life, and though she still had roses in her cheeks, it was art and not nature that put them there.

The next afternoon, while he was trying to decide what to do, a message came from Lady Bellaston. The friend's house where she had been meeting Tom was not available. They would have to meet at her own house, at seven exactly.

Tom arrived at the house a little earlier than seven, and Lady Bellaston had not yet returned from dinner. He was waiting in the hall when the door opened and in came – no other than Sophia herself. Lady Bellaston had cleverly sent her to the theatre so she could be alone with Tom, but Sophia had not enjoyed the play and had left quite early.

Sophia first went to look in a mirror. Behind her own lovely face she suddenly saw Tom. Turning to him, she screamed, and he moved forward to catch her before she fainted. To describe their looks and thoughts at this moment is beyond my power. If you have ever been in love you will feel in your own heart what passed in theirs.

In the time they had alone, Tom returned Sophia's notebook and the banknote. Then he fell to his knees and apologized to her about what had happened in the inn at Upton. Sophia was very glad to hear that he had never seen Mrs Waters again, but was angry that Tom had told people in the inn that he was escaping from Sophia's love. Tom, who was surprised at these words, was able to trace them back to Partridge, and swore more than once that he would put him to death as soon as he got home.

Things were now going so well that Tom began to say some words that sounded like a proposal of marriage, when suddenly in came Lady Bellaston.

'Miss Western,' she said, with admirable control, 'I thought you were at the theatre.'

'Miss Western,' Lady Bellaston said, with admirable control, 'I thought
you were at the theatre.'

Sophia, who had no suspicions about Tom's reason for being in the house, explained why she had come home early. Then she said that the gentleman with her had returned her notebook. Both the ladies then thanked him, and Tom, playing a very complicated game, asked for a high reward: 'It is, ladies, the honour of visiting you here again.'

'Do you know, Sophy dear,' said Lady Bellaston after Tom had left, 'I had a horrible suspicion when I first came into the room that the young gentleman was Mr Jones.'

'Indeed,' cried Sophia, laughing.

'Oh, Sophy! Sophy!' cried the lady. 'I can see by your colour that you still have Mr Jones in your thoughts.'

'On my honour, madam,' said Sophia, 'Mr Jones is as unimportant to me as the gentleman who just left us.'

'Then I promise I will not mention his name again,' said Lady Bellaston, and the two ladies went to bed, each feeling rather clever.

Sophia lay awake all night, but Lady Bellaston did not. She was enjoying her secret meetings with Tom, and next day she saw a way to remove her young rival from the scene.

Chapter 19 Tom Proposes Marriage

Sophia had another admirer, an English lord, who had met her more than once at Lady Bellaston's. He had noticed her at the theatre, and was disappointed when she left early. Next morning he called to say he hoped she was not unwell. He stayed for two hours, and in that time he fell in love. Lady Bellaston was pleased to see her noble friend paying so much attention to Sophia. She took him to one side and said, 'Lord Fellamar, are you in love with my young cousin from the country?'

'I believe I am, madam,' said Lord Fellamar. 'Will you tell her father that I wish to marry her?'

'I will indeed,' answered the lady, 'and I am sure he will agree. But there is one problem. You have a rival.'

Lord Fellamar looked disappointed.

'But,' added the lady, 'though she loves this rival, he is a beggar and a bastard. I believe you can solve this problem, but not by gentle methods.'

'What do you mean, my lady?' asked Lord Fellamar.

'If you are willing to be bold, my lord, you could be married to my cousin within a week,' said Lady Bellaston.

Lady Bellaston and Lord Fellamar then made a plan.

At seven that evening, when Sophia was alone in her room, reading a tragic novel, the door suddenly opened and in came Lord Fellamar. Sophia dropped her book, and Lord Fellamar made a low bow.

'Madam,' he said, 'as you have my heart, you cannot be surprised by a visit from its owner.'

'Are you out of your senses, my lord?' answered Sophia.

'I am, madam,' cried Lord Fellamar, taking her hand. 'You are my angel, and you must be mine.'

Sophia pulled her hand away and tried to leave, but Lord Fellamar caught her in his arms and said, 'I cannot live without you, so I must make you mine.'

'I will scream,' said Sophia, and she did, but Lady Bellaston had taken care to send the servants away.

Suddenly, an enormous noise filled the house, and help came to poor Sophia in a very unexpected way. 'Where is she?' cried the loud voice of Mr Western. 'Where is my daughter? I know she's in this house!' And the door flew open to let in Sophia's father and all his followers.

I shall never be able to describe the situation that followed, unless the reader's imagination helps me. Sophia fell into a chair, pale, frightened and full of relief. Lord Fellamar sat down near her, amazed, frightened and ashamed. Mr Western's clothes were rather untidy. He was, in plain English, drunk.

Lady Bellaston now entered the room.

After an unsteady bow, Mr Western said, 'Sophy, here is your cousin. In front of her, won't you tell me that you will marry one of the best young men in England?'

'Sir,' said Lord Fellamar, thinking Mr Western meant him. 'I am the happy man who will marry your daughter.'

'You are a son of the devil,' shouted Western. 'She will not marry you, in spite of your fine clothes. Come, madam!'

And Mr Western rushed his daughter into a carriage and ordered it to drive to his lodgings. When her maid, Honour, tried to come too, he refused, saying, 'No more escapes, Sophy. I will get you a better maid.'

◆

Luckily, Honour knew where to find Tom, and she went straight to his lodgings to tell him what had happened. She had no idea how Mr Western had found Sophia, or where he had taken her.

In fact, Harriet Fitzpatrick had written to her aunt, Mrs Western, to tell her that Sophia was in London, staying with Lady Bellaston. As soon as she received the letter, Mrs Western told her brother where to find his lost sheep. He immediately sent word to Mr Allworthy and Mr Blifil, told his servants to get the horses ready and set off for London, taking Mr Supple, the priest, with him.

◆

Fortune seemed determined to be Tom's enemy. He now had two rivals, and once again he had lost his dear Sophia.

Tom now tried to avoid Lady Bellaston, but letters from her were delivered every hour. When his friend Nightingale saw how worried Tom was, he wanted to help him.

'Dear Tom,' said Nightingale. 'Are you troubled by the Queen of the Fairies? Oh, please don't be angry with me for mentioning what the whole town knows. Are you in love with her?'

Tom sighed and said, 'No, my friend, but I owe so much to her that I don't know how to end our affair.'

'You are not the first young man she has captured like this,' said Nightingale, 'so you needn't worry about her reputation. But as you are a man of honour, let me tell you a way. Propose marriage to her.'

'Marriage!' cried Tom.

'Yes, marriage,' answered Nightingale. 'She will refuse.'

Nightingale persuaded Tom that there was no danger that the lady would accept his proposal, so he wrote her a charming letter. He soon received a short answer.

Sir: I see your purpose. You wish me to put my whole fortune in your power. Do you imagine that I am a fool? If you come to my house again I shall not be at home.

'Well,' said Nightingale, 'you now have your freedom!'

Tom could not thank him enough.

Chapter 20 A Kidnapping is Planned

Mr Western took Sophia to his lodgings in Piccadilly and once again asked her to agree to marry Mr Blifil. When she refused, he locked her in her room and put the key in his own pocket. He swore he would not let her out until she promised to marry Blifil.

Lord Fellamar sent an apology to Mr Western, and asked for permission to visit his daughter as a lover. The messenger took the opportunity to tell Mr Western about his lord's great position and fortune. To this, Western said: 'Look, sir, my daughter's marriage is already arranged, but if it was not, I would never marry her to a lord. I hate all lords and will have nothing to do with them.' He then kicked the man out with shouts and curses.

In her prison room above, Sophia also began to kick and shout. Her father immediately ran upstairs, unlocked the door, and found her pale and breathless.

'Oh, my dear sir,' she said. 'I was so frightened by all that loud noise. What happened? Were you hurt?'

'Just a quarrel about you, Sophy. All my misfortunes are about you. Come, do be a good girl. Blifil will be here in a day or two. Make me the happiest man in the world and I will make you the happiest woman. You shall have the finest clothes in London, the finest jewels and a carriage with six horses. I promised Allworthy to give you half of my property when you marry, and you shall have the other half when I die. You are my only joy on earth, my little Sophy.'

Mr Western had tears in his eyes, and so did Sophia. 'Do you really wish me to be happy, dear father? Then let me marry nobody. Let me come home and be your Sophy again.'

'No, Sophy,' he cried in a voice like thunder. 'You *will* marry Blifil. You *will* have him even if you hang yourself the next morning!' And he marched out of the room, leaving his poor, terrified daughter in a flood of tears.

◆

Mr Western had brought several servants to town with him, and among them was his favourite, the gamekeeper Black George. Meals were taken regularly to Sophia's room, but she ate very little, so when Black George asked his master if he could tempt her with a little cooked chicken, Mr Western agreed. They went upstairs together, Mr Western unlocked the door and Black George carried in her dinner. He told Sophia that the chicken was full of eggs, and left it on her table.

Sophia was very fond of eggs, so when she was alone again she opened the chicken. It was full of eggs. There was also a letter which had not been put there by Nature, but as the result of a lucky meeting in the street between Partridge and Black George that morning.

Sophia immediately tore open the letter and read it. It told her that her Tom loved her, that his arms were ready to receive her if she wanted to escape, but that if she decided to make peace with her father by forgetting her lover, he would understand.

Now a new noise came from downstairs. Mr Western was arguing loudly with his sister, who had just arrived.

'How can you lock up your daughter,' cried Mrs Western. 'Have I not often told you that women in a free country cannot be treated like this? We are as free as men. You must let me take my niece with me to my own lodgings. These rooms are not fit for a woman of quality.'

Mr Western finally agreed. He did not want his sister to change her will and leave her wealth to somebody else.

◆

From her aunt's lodgings, Sophia managed to send a reply to Tom's letter. He spent three hours reading and kissing it, for it told him she would never marry another man. It also said she had promised her aunt not to see or talk to him.

When Blifil arrived in London, Mr Western took him straight to see Sophia. To their surprise, her aunt was a little cool. She told them it was not polite to come so early in the day, and sent them away until the afternoon.

Actually, she had another reason for delaying Blifil's visit. She wanted to visit Lady Bellaston and find out more about the lord who wanted to marry Sophia. What she heard about him from her cousin was very satisfactory indeed.

Lady Bellaston now had every reason to hate Sophia, and she told Mrs Western a secret. 'This will make you laugh,' she said.

'Would you believe that young Jones tried to make love to me? Look, here is a letter he wrote me.' And she passed her Tom's letter with the proposal of marriage.

'I am astonished,' said Mrs Western. 'Whatever did you do with this fellow?'

'Whatever I did, I do not want him as a husband,' laughed Lady Bellaston. 'I tried that once, and once is enough for any reasonable woman. Please take the letter, if you think you can use it.'

When her cousin had left with the letter, Lady Bellaston received Lord Fellamar, who was still determined to win Sophia for himself. He told her about the way his messenger had been treated by Sophia's father.

Lady Bellaston simply laughed. She told him the father was a country fellow not worth worrying about. His sister, Mrs Western, would persuade him to accept the lord's proposal. The real problem was the young bastard whom Sophia loved.

'Perhaps, my lord,' she suggested, 'you could find some way to remove him? Kidnap him, perhaps? Send him to sea? I could tell you where he lives, if you wish to know.'

Chapter 21 Mr Western Sings for Joy

It was now that Fortune really deserted our hero. He received an unexpected invitation from Mrs Fitzpatrick, who perhaps wanted to try what Lady Bellaston no longer wanted.

By now Harriet thought herself safe from her husband, who had gone to look for her in Bath. But when she had written to tell Mrs Western where to look for Sophia, her aunt had told Mr Fitzpatrick where to look for his wife.

It was chance that brought Tom to Harriet Fitzpatrick's door just as her husband appeared on the scene. It was jealousy that persuaded Mr Fitzpatrick that Tom had been making love to his wife. And it was temper that made him strike Tom on the head and pull out his sword.

Tom was amazed, pulled out his own sword and drove half of it into the gentleman's body. Now it was Fitzpatrick's turn to look amazed. 'I am a dead man,' he cried.

A gang of rough men rushed up to get hold of Tom. These were Lord Fellamar's men, who had been following Tom, waiting for a chance to kidnap him.

'Well, Jack,' laughed one of them. 'He's not going to sea now. He's going somewhere worse, when that man dies.'

Similar jokes were made about Tom until a doctor came to look at Fitzpatrick and the police arrived to arrest Tom. The doctor said he believed Fitzpatrick would die, so Tom was taken to a prison.

Partridge found him there next morning. He brought the news that Fitzpatrick was dead, and a letter from Sophia, which Black George had passed to him. It said:

My aunt has just shown me a letter which you wrote to Lady Bellaston. I never want to hear your name again. SW

◆

Fortune now threatens to see our hero hanged in public, and if our reader enjoys such scenes, I think he should book a seat in the first row now. This I faithfully promise: if he does not find some natural means to escape a sad end, I will not help him with unnatural means. You can trust me not to bring in gods or spirits or fairies.

We must now return to Mrs Miller's house, where Mr Allworthy had arrived with his nephew, Blifil. Mrs Miller wanted to change Mr Allworthy's view of Tom, his adopted son. She told him how Tom had given money to her cousin.

'He always speaks lovingly of you, sir,' she said.

'You surprise me, madam,' said Mr Allworthy. 'You have not seen the side of him which shocks my nephew and myself.'

'I see only that he has enemies,' said Mrs Miller, 'but what they say of him cannot be true.'

At this moment, Blifil came in from the street with an excited look on his face. 'What do you think, sir,' he cried. 'I am sorry to be the one to bring such bad news. Mr Jones, to whom you were so very good, has killed a man.'

Allworthy looked shocked. He turned to Mrs Miller and cried, 'Well, madam, what do you say now?'

'I say, sir, that if it is true, the man he killed must be at fault. I never saw a man so kind, and so sweet-tempered as Mr Jones. He was loved by every one in this house, and every one who came near it.'

They were interrupted by a loud knocking at the door. It was Mr Western. 'Neighbour,' he cried, as he entered the room. 'All this time we have been afraid of a young bastard and now there is the devil of a lord, who may be a bastard too for all I care. But he will never have my daughter!'

It took some time for Mr Allworthy to find out what Mr Western meant. Lady Bellaston and Mrs Western had been trying to persuade him not to refuse Lord Fellamar's offer.

When Mr Allworthy understood the situation, he instantly told Mr Western that Sophia should never be forced to marry Blifil against her will. If she chose to marry the lord, he wished her every happiness in this noble marriage.

'She will marry Blifil,' said Mr Western, 'for three reasons. First, is she not my child? Second, do I not govern my own child? And third, am I asking her to do anything for me? No, it is to make her happy!'

Blifil now spoke. 'Mr Western is very kind to prefer me to Lord Fellamar,' he said. 'While I would never wish to win his daughter by violence, perhaps her heart will be free when she hears that Mr Jones is in prison for murder.'

'What's that?' cried Western. 'Murder! Is he a murderer, and is there any chance of seeing him hanged? I have never heard better news in my life! Tol de rol, tol-lol de rol,' and he sang and danced about the room.

◆

Several true friends now came to visit Tom in prison. First, the faithful Partridge came to tell him that Mr Fitzpatrick was still alive.

Then Nightingale came, with Mrs Miller. 'Even if the fellow dies,' he said, 'you will not hang. It was an accident, because he attacked you first.'

'Yes, he did,' sighed Tom, 'but I do not want to be responsible for another man's death. And there is something else that makes me miserable.'

'Come, come, Mr Jones,' said Mrs Miller, who had heard from Partridge about Sophia's letter to Tom. 'Things will be better soon. Mr Blifil has no chance with the lady.'

Tom asked the good woman to take a letter to Sophia, which she did, and there were tears on Sophia's pillow that night.

Chapter 22 The Truth Comes Out

Before we return to Tom we will take one more look at Sophia. Her aunt could not understand why she did not want to bring honour on her family by marrying Lord Fellamar.

'Don't you want a noble name?' she asked.

Sophia did not. 'He behaved so rudely,' she explained. 'I am almost ashamed to tell you. He caught me in his arms, pulled me down, put his hand into my dress and kissed my breast with such violence that I have a mark there still.'

'Indeed!' said Mrs Western.

'Yes, indeed, madam,' said Sophia. 'Luckily my father came in at that moment.'

'I am astonished,' cried her aunt. 'It is an insult! I have had lovers, many lovers, but no man kissed more of me than my cheek. Oh, I was cruel. I refused them all.'

'Then, dear aunt, will you not let me refuse this one?'

Mrs Western did agree that Sophia might be a little cool to Lord Fellamar, and Sophia hoped she could now persuade him that it was useless to pursue her. But an unfortunate accident happened which made her aunt furious again.

Sophia's maid saw Tom's letter, and told Mrs Western.

'Miss Western!' her aunt cried. 'I hear you have received a letter! A letter from a murderer! I am disgusted! I shall return you to your father tomorrow morning!'

◆

The next time Nightingale visited Tom in prison he had some bad news. 'I have heard,' he said, 'that the gang of men who saw you fight with Mr Fitzpatrick are ready to tell the judge that you hit him first.'

'Then they lie,' exclaimed Tom. 'Why would they do that?'

Mrs Miller then arrived to say she had delivered Tom's letter, but when she returned for a reply, Sophia had gone.

Tom said he now had no interest in life and was ready to meet God. After his death, his name might be cleared.

A guard then brought in a message from a lady who wished to see Tom. His friends left, and the lady was sent in.

Tom was astonished to see that it was Mrs Waters!

The reader will remember that Mrs Waters left the inn at Upton in a carriage with Mr Fitzpatrick and his friend, and travelled to Bath in their company. As Mrs Fitzpatrick had run away, Mr Fitzpatrick took the opportunity to examine Mrs

Tom was astonished to see that it was Mrs Waters!

Waters carefully, and he decided to offer her the position of wife. She accepted, and lived with him in Bath.

Mrs Waters had come to London with Mr Fitzpatrick without knowing the reason for his visit. He had never mentioned a wife to her, and he had never mentioned the name of Jones. It was only when he was getting better that he told her the story of the fight. She had brought some good news for Tom.

'By an amazing chance,' she said, 'I know the man you hurt, Mr Jones, and I promise you that he is not dying. He will also tell the judge that he struck the first blow.'

This unexpected news made Tom very happy, and he enjoyed talking with Mrs Waters for a little longer, and laughing about their adventures at Upton.

Just after Mrs Waters left, Partridge came into the room with a white face. He had been in the next room, listening.

'Oh, sir,' he said. 'Was that the woman you were with at Upton? Did you really go to bed with her? Oh, sir, may God forgive you. That woman was Jenny Jones. You have been to bed with your own mother!'

Tom became a picture of horror. For a time, the two men stared wildly at each other. Then Tom begged Partridge to run after Mrs Waters, but she had disappeared.

Some hours later a note came from Mrs Waters. It said that she had just learned who he was, and she had something important to tell him as soon as she could see him again.

◆

It was now that Mr Allworthy began to have some unexpected visitors. The first was Partridge.

'You are a strange fellow,' said Mr Allworthy to the schoolteacher. 'Why are you the servant of your own son?'

'I am not his servant, sir,' replied Partridge. 'Nor am I his father. And I wish, sir, that his mother were not his mother.' He then told Mr Allworthy the whole story.

Mr Allworthy was as shocked as Partridge himself. Then Mrs Waters came hurrying into the room.

'There, sir, is Jenny Jones, the mother of Mr Jones. She will tell you that I am not his father,' cried Partridge.

'He is not,' said Mrs Waters. 'You will remember, sir, that I promised you would know one day who the baby's father was. Now, if we may talk alone, I am here to tell you.' Partridge left them, and she began her story.

'Sir,' she said. 'You will remember a young man called Summer, who lived as a student in your house, and died very young. He was a handsome fellow, and very good-natured.'

'Indeed, I do remember him,' said Mr Allworthy. 'Was he the father of your son?'

'He was not, sir. He was the father of the child, but I am not his mother, and I am glad of it.'

'Be careful not to lie,' said Mr Allworthy, coldly.

'I did help when the child was born,' she said, 'and I put him in your bed, but the baby was your sister's child.'

'My sister, Bridget?' he cried. 'Can it be possible?'

'Have patience, sir, and I will tell you her sad story.'

Mr Allworthy listened with astonishment to the story of how his sister Bridget loved Summers, and how they hoped to marry, but were prevented by his sudden death. Bridget had then asked Jenny Jones to help her have her baby in secret.

'But why,' asked Allworthy, 'did she carry this secret with her out of the world?'

'I am sure she did not,' said Mrs Waters. 'She knew you loved her son, and always said she would tell you.'

'I must speak to her lawyer,' said Mr Allworthy.

Now that busy fellow, Mr Dowling, whose work took him up and down the country, was in London, helping Mr Blifil with some business. Mr Allworthy sent for him at once. When she saw

83

him, Mrs Waters looked surprised, but she said nothing.

'Mr Dowling,' said Mr Allworthy, 'I have just found out that Mr Jones is my own nephew.'

'Indeed, sir, I know,' said Mr Dowling.

'Then why did you never mention it?'

'Well, sir, as you did not mention it, I thought you wished to hide it from the world.'

'I did not know,' cried Mr Allworthy. 'How could I?'

'By reading the letter that I brought from your sister the night she died. The letter that I gave to Mr Blifil.'

'Heavens,' said Mr Allworthy. 'I never saw that letter.'

Mrs Waters now spoke. 'I am surprised, sir, that if this gentleman knew that Mr Jones was your nephew, he would want to see him hanged. Did you know, sir, that he visited Mr Fitzpatrick and offered him money to swear that Mr Jones had struck him first?'

'I did not,' said Mr Allworthy. 'Is this true?'

'It is true, sir,' said Mr Dowling. 'Mr Blifil sent me to offer a bribe to Mr Fitzpatrick, and another to the men who saw the fight.'

'I am astonished,' said Mr Allworthy. 'Send for Blifil. And tell him to bring the letter which his mother wrote me on her deathbed. I will see him when I return.'

Chapter 23 The Story Reaches its Conclusion

Mr Allworthy now went to Mr Western's and asked to see Sophia. After some moments of silence, he began to speak.

'I am afraid, Miss Western, that my family has made you most unhappy, and I believe I must blame myself. When your father and I agreed to your marriage to Mr Blifil, I did not know as much about him as I do now. I wish to release you from the arrangement.'

Sophia was more grateful than she could say.

'I have another proposal,' he continued. 'I have a young relation of very good character, and I will give him the fortune I planned to give to Mr Blifil. Would you allow my relation to visit you?'

Sophia, after a minute's silence, answered, 'I have decided to listen to no such proposals at present, sir, but to return to Somerset to take care of my father.'

'Then, Miss Western,' replied Mr Allworthy. 'My relation must continue to suffer disappointment.'

Sophia smiled. 'Can he suffer if he does not know me?'

'Indeed he knows you,' said Mr Allworthy, 'for he is my own nephew, Mr Jones.'

'Can it be possible?' cried Sophia.

'Indeed, madam, he is my own sister's son. Oh, Miss Western, I have treated him cruelly. I shall never be able to reward him for his sufferings without your help. Will you not see him? I know he has faults, but I believe he has those good qualities which will make him a good husband.'

At this point, Mr Western joined them. 'See here,' he cried, 'I have a letter from my cousin, Lady Bellaston. She says that murderer, Jones, has got out of prison, and I should lock up my daughter again. Neighbour, you don't know what trouble daughters are.'

'Mr Western,' said Mr Allworthy, 'I shall return now to see Mr Jones at my lodgings, and invite you to follow.'

◆

It is impossible to imagine a more tender or moving scene than the meeting between uncle and nephew. It is beyond my power to describe the joy that was felt on both sides. After Mr Allworthy had lifted Tom from his feet, where he had thrown himself, he held him in his arms and cried: 'Oh, my child, how I have been to blame for my unkind suspicions and the sufferings they have caused you.'

'I have not been punished more than I deserve,' said Tom.

Mr Allworthy then told Tom all he knew about Blifil, and promised to give him all that he needed to make him happy.

'I owe everything to your great goodness, dear Uncle,' said Tom. 'But, sir, there is one sadness which I must confess to you. I have lost my angel.'

Here the conversation was interrupted by the arrival of Western, who had heard the news from Sophia and could not wait to see Tom.

'My old friend,' he cried out, 'I am glad to see you, with all my heart. All the past must be forgotten. We must forgive each other. I'll take you to my Sophy this moment.'

As Tom dressed for his visit to Sophia, Partridge was so full of joy that he made a dozen mistakes. 'I always told you, sir,' he laughed, 'that one day you would have it in your power to make my fortune.' Tom happily agreed.

♦

And now Tom went to Mr Western's with his uncle. He was, indeed, a very fine sight. Sophia had also dressed carefully, and looked so extremely beautiful that Allworthy whispered to Western that she was the finest sight in the world.

They all had tea, and then the lovers were left alone.

It was strange that two people who had so much to say to each other when there was danger, and who so wanted to rush into each other's arms when there were barriers, were now quiet and still. They were now safe and free to say or do what they pleased, but they sat in perfect silence.

At last Tom said, 'Oh, my Sophia, you know all about me now. Can I ever hope for forgiveness?'

'You must forgive yourself, Mr Jones,' she replied.

'Then will you believe that my wicked ways are behind me now?' he begged.

'I will never marry a man whose word I cannot trust,' she answered. 'Could you be faithful, after what I know?'

Tom took her hand and pulled her to the mirror. 'Look there, my charming angel,' he cried. 'Look at that lovely face, that shape, those eyes and that mind that shines through those eyes. There is my proof. For what man who has these could be unfaithful?'

'Then, perhaps, Mr Jones,' said Sophia shyly, 'we could talk about marriage.'

'Say when, my Sophia,' cried Tom. 'Love is impatient.'

'Perhaps in twelve months,' said Sophia sweetly, and Tom took her in his arms and kissed her with a passion he had never felt before.

At this moment, Mr Western burst into the room, and with his hunting voice cried out, 'Go to her, boy! That's it, my honeys! Well, is it agreed? Will you marry tomorrow?'

'No, no,' cried Sophia, 'not tomorrow.'

'Yes, yes,' cried her father. 'Will you disobey me?'

'Then,' said Sophia, 'if my father wishes it, yes.'

Her father called Mr Allworthy. 'Good news, neighbour,' he shouted. 'We'll have a wedding tomorrow, and I bet you five pounds we will have a baby boy nine months from tomorrow!'

◆

And so, reader, all ended well for our hero, our heroine and their faithful friends. And when Mr Western became the grandfather of two fine babies, a boy and a girl, he told the world that their childish voices were sweeter to him than the music of all the hunting dogs in England.

ACTIVITIES

Chapters 1–4

Before you read

1 Read the opening lines of the Introduction. What 'crimes' might an energetic young teenager commit?

2 Find these words in your dictionary. The words are all in the story.

   bastard Bible fellow fortune furious gamekeeper
   hang honour naked nearby

   Which word means:
   a without clothes?
   b very angry?
   c good luck?
   d in the area?
   e to die with a rope around your neck?
   f a man?
   g a child of unmarried parents?
   h high standards of behaviour?
   i the Christian holy book?
   j a man who protects wild animals for hunting?

After you read

3 Who:
   a has 'good health, good sense and a kind heart'?
   b 'often thanked God she was not beautiful'?
   c 'behaved in a superior way'?
   d is 'in love with Mr Allworthy's house, gardens, villages and farms'?
   e 'attacked her husband with tongue, teeth and hands'?
   f is 'a perfect lady'?
   g 'had a natural way with ladies'?
   h is 'one of the best-looking girls in the whole country'?

4 Compare the characters of Tom Jones and Master Blifil. Is it surprising that they are not friends?

Chapters 5–8

Before you read

5 Tom is in a difficult situation. How do you think he is going to get out of it?

6 Answer questions about these new words.
   a If you leave someone money in your *will*, when do they get it?
   b If you *disgrace* your family, how do they feel?

7 Answer these questions.

   a Why does Mr Western want his daughter to marry Blifil?

   b Why can Tom not be considered a suitable husband?

8 Imagine that you are Sophia. Explain why you still love Tom, although you suspect that he has been close to Molly.

Chapters 9–13
Before you read

9 Will Sophia obey her father? What do you think will happen if she continues to refuse?

10 Find these words in your dictionary.

   barber   inn   maid   rage   sword

   Which words refer to:

   a an emotion?   **c** people?

   b a building?   **d** a fighting tool?

After you read

11 Who says these words? Who to? What are they talking about?

   a 'My death would have made us both happier.'

   b 'If I catch him, I'll kill him.'

   c 'I was just having a joke.'

   d '. . . you have been my greatest enemy.'

   e 'You must be a good angel.'

12 Work in pairs. Act out one of these conversations, using your own words.

   a Mr Allworthy is talking to Tom. He has heard about Tom's fight in the fields.

   b Mr Partridge is telling Tom how he knows him.

Chapters 14–18
Before you read

13 The situation at the inn is now going to become even more complicated. How is that possible, do you think?

14 Answer questions about these definitions.

   a 'A British lord is a man with a title that he has been given by the king or queen or that his father had before him.'

Do you have titles like this in your country? Who uses them? Do they bring respect?

b 'You wear a mask over all or part of your face to hide it.'

Are there occasions in your country when it is common to wear a mask? Are there times when it is useful?

After you read

15 Why are these objects important to the story?

  a a ring on a pillow

  b a banknote in the road

  c a mask with an invitation

16 Discuss the humour in these chapters. Do you find Tom's adventures amusing? Which characters do you find funny?

Chapters 19–23

Before you read

17 Read this sentence from the next part of the story.

'. . . Tom took her in his arms and kissed her with a passion he had never felt before.'

  a Who do you think Tom is kissing now?

  b What does the word *passion* mean?

  c Why has he never felt such passion before?

After you read

18 What part does Lord Fellamar play in the story?

19 Tom is very attractive to women and has not been able to resist them. Sophia has forgiven him for this. Discuss whether she is right.

Writing

20 '*Tom Jones* is a mixture of love, adventure and comedy.' Describe a scene which is a good example of this mixture. Explain why you enjoyed it.

21 Imagine that you are Mr Western. Reply to a letter from one of your grandchildren asking how his/her father came to marry their mother.

22 Write about the role that one of these characters plays in the story: Jenny Jones   Blifil   Lady Bellaston

23 Discuss the different views of marriage that are held by characters in the book. Which views do you share?